THE TRAIL TO YUMA

by

Terrell L. Bowers

Dales Large Print Books
Long Preston, North Yorkshire,
BD23 4ND, England.

British Library Cataloguing in Publication Data.

Bowers, Terrell L.
    The trail to Yuma.

    A catalogue record of this book is
    available from the British Library

    ISBN   978-1-84262-591-0 pbk

First published in Great Britain in 2007 by Robert Hale Limited

Copyright © Terrell L. Bowers 2007

Cover illustration © Gordon Crabb by arrangement with
Alison Eldred

The right of Terrell L. Bowers to be identified as the author of
this work has been asserted by him in accordance with the
Copyright, Designs and Patents Act, 1988

Published in Large Print 2008 by arrangement with
Robert Hale Ltd.

Dales Large Print is an imprint of Library Magna Books Ltd.

Printed and bound in Great Britain by
T.J. (International) Ltd., Cornwall, PL28 8RW

CHAPTER ONE

Steamboat travel between San Francisco to Yuma was nothing like the floating palaces along the Mississippi River. Traversing with the current, the trip might be accomplished in as little as three days. Going upstream, when the water was either running low or unusually high, the trip could take two weeks or more. This particular trip fell into the latter category as the river-banks were several feet below the average waterline.

Clay Valenteen had never made the trip before, but he had gleaned information from a one-time crew member and picked up a tip or two. During the heat of summer, the temperature aboard ship often topped 120 degrees. Drinking water became warm and tepid, while stored lard and butter turned as liquid as lamp oil. The heat caused supplies to spoil quickly and soon the storage section permeated that section of the ship with the smell of rotted food. On the longer trips up-river, even the hardiest of travelers suffered bouts of ill-effects from the poor food and tainted water.

This trip was in August and once the food began to smell, Clay ate only from his own meager store of jerky, hard rolls and airtights of beans. It left him hungry most of the time, but he maintained his health.

Daily survival was a chore until the sun finally dipped over the horizon. Once night covered the land the temperature would drop twenty degrees or more. It was like a new day. A man could actually take a deep breath or venture a walk out on deck. Clay chose such a night, when the darkness and cooler temperature afforded him a chance to slip down to the hold of the ship to inspect several crates.

With no windows or portals, the storage compartment was as dark as a layer of tar. Valenteen warily entered the hold and paused to strike and put a match to a candle he had procured on board. It was a small candle and didn't put off much light, but it allowed him to see well enough to move about. The boxes and bags being transported were stacked to distribute the weight of the load evenly across the hull. After a short search Clay located the rectangular boxes he'd been looking for. The black printing on the side of the crates read Farm Tools. The destination was Yuma and the tag read consigned to Warren Locke. Clay set the candle on an adjacent box and began to pry open one corner.

'What are you doing, drummer?' a hostile voice challenged from the cargo bay door. Clay spun about to face a burly built man. Even in the subdued light, he could make out a malevolent expression on the intruder's ugly puss. Before he could answer, the man produced a huge skinning knife.

'Whoa! There's no cause to get riled, fella,' Clay spoke with a calm he didn't feel. 'I'm only trying to find my gear.'

The brute sneered, 'Your gear ain't in the box you was fixing to open just now.'

'I was only–'

But the big man lunged forward and took a vicious swipe with his blade that nearly removed Clay's left eye!

Clay jumped back. 'Hey!' he hollered, lifting his hands to ward off the man's attack. 'What's gotten into you, mister? Are you crazy?'

The bruiser didn't answer. He rushed at Clay, skirting the boxes, trying to get at him. Clay was more fleet of foot and adroitly kept his distance. Twice around the hold, scrambling over and around boxes, the brute stopped the chase to catch his breath. He used the back of his hand to mop his perspiring brow.

'I've been watching you, drummer,' he panted, sucking in gulps of the stagnant air. 'You're too durned nosy to be a salesman.'

'You're wrong, my friend. I work for–'

But the heavy-set man had been feigning his weakness. He made a wild lunge over the boxes. Clay spun away, but the fellow's hand caught hold of his shirt and dragged him to the floor. The slashing blade of the knife came down in a vicious arc–

Clay rolled to the side in time to avoid being stabbed. He kicked free and crawled away.

The powerful man pawed after him, trying to grab his ankles, but Clay scrambled to his feet and backed up a couple steps. He drew his snub-nosed .44 Colt Army revolver from its holster and pointed it at the man's chest.

'All right,' he warned, 'time to calm down, mister, before I feed you a few ounces of lead!'

Rather than back off, the burly brute lifted the knife and charged at him like an enraged bear. Clay swung the pistol like a club, but the brute's body slammed into him and they went down in a tangle. He spied the knife lift upward, another attempt to drive home the blade.

Clay did not hesitate a second time, he pulled the trigger of his gun.

The muffled explosion didn't sound like something that would inflict a fatal wound, but it stopped the giant's attack in mid-motion. A guttural groan escaped his lips, as the knife slipped from his fingers and he fell onto his side. Valenteen struggled out from under his weight, when a second shadow darted out from behind a stack of crates.

Valenteen coiled like a spring and dove for the fleeing phantom. His fingers grabbed a handful of trousers and he dragged the phantom to the floor. Before the smaller man could escape, Valenteen climbed astraddle the boy and pointed his gun at a young, terrified face.

'Hold it, you little sidewinder!' he told the squirming prisoner.

'No, *you* hold it!' a stern voice snapped from the doorway.

Several men appeared at the entrance to the cargo hold. They had obviously heard the gunshot and come to investigate. Clay lowered his gun at once.

'Get some light in here!' the captain bellowed. He pointed his finger at Clay and the youth he had pinned beneath his body. 'You two stay put!'

Clay remained sitting atop the young man's stomach while he holstered his pistol and raised his hands. He didn't intend to get himself killed by some nervous seaman. He would tell what happened and hope the human seat cushion under him would back up his story. The boy had probably been in a good position to see what had transpired. Once he told the captain how Clay had only defended himself, the incident would be forgotten.

Clay put an icy glare on the youngster who called himself Billy. They were separated by some fifteen feet, each chained at the left wrist to an opposite wall of a cabin. The boy kept his head lowered, hiding his face beneath a big, floppy, farmer's hat. His clothes were ragged, caked with dirt, and when Clay had managed a glimpse of his face, it was smudged with sweat and grime. He reeked of spoiled potatoes, having evidently picked up the smell from his hiding place near a food locker. Clay gritted his teeth and wished he were free long enough so he might grab the boy by the collar and shake some sense into him.

'You slippery, no-good, back-stabbing little weasel!' Clay exploded. 'What's the idea of not backing my story? You saw what happened down in the cargo hold. That big oaf was about to carve me a new gizzard!'

'I didn't see nuthen,' Billy muttered.

Clay reined in his temper. 'You're a stow-away, son. The most they will do to you is take you back to wherever you stowed aboard. I'm looking at a rope around my neck!'

'You killed him,' was the soft reply.

'It was him or me! You can't be so blind and stupid as to not understand the differ-ence between murder and self-defense!'

The boy kept his head lowered, refusing to meet Clay's smoldering stare. The hat was pulled down over his ears and the heavy coveralls were so long they covered up most of his shoes. The baggy pants hid his actual size, but he'd been as easy to throw and pin as a newborn calf.

'You a farmer?' Clay tried a new approach. If he couldn't scare the kid into telling the truth, perhaps he could reason with him.

'Was,' came the simple answer.

'Where you from?'

'Down-river.'

Clay sighed at his elusive response.

'My name is Clay Valenteen. I'm a sales representative for The Original Grange Supply House. Ever hear of it?'

The head nodded ever so slightly.

'So what's your last name?'

There was a slight hesitation. 'It's just Billy.'

Clay tried again. 'How old are you, Billy?'

After a slight hesitation, 'Sixteen ... last month.'

'Well, Billy, you can do me a good turn by telling the captain what you saw in the hold. Maybe I can return the favor.'

'I'm not looking for favors,' Billy said flatly.

Clay clenched his teeth, but maintained his poise. He removed his flat-crowned John B. hat, trying to think of a new angle. He felt the sting beneath the iron bracelet on his left wrist, caused by perspiration against chaffed skin. He didn't relish the idea of being shackled for the duration of the trip.

Using the hat to fan his face, he tried again. 'If you admit what you saw, they might release you until we reach Yuma,' Clay tried a new approach. 'They have a territorial judge there.'

'I'm not saying anything,' was the youth's curt reply.

Clay silently imagined strangling the little squirt, but he kept his voice mellow. 'How do you intend to pay the ninety-dollar fare for your trip up here?'

Billy shrugged his slight shoulders.

'The captain will likely keep you aboard and take you back down-river with him.'

'If he does, I'll jump ship and swim to shore. I won't go back to–' the sentence was cut short. He had almost slipped and mentioned where he'd come from.

'I'm not asking you to lie for me, Billy,' Clay said gently. 'All you have to do is tell what you saw and heard down in the hold. I'm no murderer. I tried to talk to the guy; it was self-defense, him or me.'

But Billy kept his face hidden by the brim of the old louse cage. It was not the kind of reaction to get over-confident about. If the kid didn't speak up to back his story, Clay could be in deep trouble.

The informal hearing was called to order shortly after sunset, presided over by the steamboat captain. Most of the crew and other passengers were present. Some sat on barrels, others on buckets or stools, while a few lounged about on the wooden deck. Billy and Clay were seated on a splintery bench, Clay with his hands bound behind him. Billy was neither chained nor bound

13

for the hearing, as his only crime was stowing away aboard the ship.

'This here is to decide what is to be done with you, Valenteen,' the captain spoke in an authoritative voice, quieting the idle chatter of the spectators. 'We must decide if you are a threat to others aboard and determine if you're telling the truth about the death of Lard Ackers.'

Valenteen met the man with a level gaze. 'I shot the man in self-defense, Captain. He attacked me with a knife.'

The captain made a negative gesture. 'A thorough search was made of the hold, Mr Valenteen. No weapon was found.'

Although the temperature was ninety-plus degrees, Clay felt a cold sweat envelope his body. His glance swept over the men on deck. He lingered a single moment on the single familiar face in the crowd and evaluated the rest. They were hard men, some downright unsavory, all dirty from travel, most unshaven, with the sweet stench of body odor. Some regarded the proceedings with a morbid curiosity, others were more serious, while a few appeared bored by the whole affair.

'May I ask who took charge of the body?' he queried the captain.

'Mort Lindsay,' he replied, tipping his

head toward one of the men.

'Lard Ackers was a friend of mine,' Mort spoke up. He rose to his feet, as if to give his testimony. 'I searched for that knife you claim Lard had on him, but it wasn't in the cargo section. I figure there never was no knife. Lard was big enough that he never needed to carry a weapon.'

The statement had leverage with the group. A big, powerfully built man like Lard, it rang true that he wouldn't have needed a knife in a fight.

'Did anyone help you search for the knife?'

Mort instantly bridled. 'You calling me a liar, drummer?'

'I'm only thinking you maybe didn't look as closely as an unbiased man might have.'

He snarled sarcastically, 'Oh, so I took the knife and hid it or threw it overboard?'

'Thanks for clearing that up,' Clay replied, turning the question into a statement.

A few spectators chuckled at the comment, while Mort's face darkened with rage. 'You kilt my friend in cold blood, Valenteen, and you're going to pay for it!'

'I'm sorry I had to kill the man,' Clay turned deadly serious, 'but Lard came at me with a knife. I warned him to stop, but he attacked and I had to shoot.'

'What does the stowaway have to say?' the familiar man spoke up. 'He must have witnessed what happened.'

'I agree,' the captain said, looking at the boy. 'You were in the hold, sonny. Tell us what you saw.'

Billy's head remained lowered enough to hide most of his face.

When he did not offer to speak, the captain warned, 'Being stowaway is against the law, young man. You're going to end up in jail or working for your passage until your debt is paid. You understand that?'

The boy's head bobbed slightly, but still he said nothing. Clay noticed his small, dirty hands were locked in front of him, as if in prayer – no doubt ready to plead for mercy.

'This man says that Lard Ackers pulled a knife on him,' the captain tried again. 'He says that he killed Lard in self-defense. You were down there in the hold: what did you see?'

'I didn't see anything,' the boy muttered.

'You had to have heard that guy threaten me,' Clay challenged the youth. 'And you sure heard me warn him to back off when I pulled my gun!'

The boy gave his head a negative shake.

'Looks like you'll stand trial for murder in

Yuma, Valenteen,' the captain announced. 'I don't envy you. The judge there is Delbert Stickley. He's one tough *hombre*. Considering how Mr Ackers had fifty pounds on you, he might let you off with twenty years hard labor. If he don't like your looks, you could find yourself on the wrong end of a rope.'

Clay glared at the young stowaway, but the boy refused to meet his eyes. There was no logic to his silence, yet his lack of support might condemn Clay to the gallows. His untimely brawl with Lard had turned from an act of self-defense to one knotted up mess.

'That's right, Marshal. I'm Captain Jack Mellon of the Colorado Steam Navigation Company. This here is the man who killed Lard Ackers. We had to put to shore long enough to bury the body down-river a few miles. This August heat would have caused that corpse to ripen in a matter of hours. Wasn't much doubt about the cause of death and Mort Lindsay, his pal on board, said he didn't have any kin here in Yuma.'

Clay stood before Will Baxter, hands tied at his back and tried to size up the town marshal. If he was honest and his own man, there might still be a chance to have this settled without causing more fuss.

'I knew Lard Ackers,' the marshal said, returning Clay's scrutiny, as if attempting to judge his character. 'He usually carried a skinning knife.'

The captain shrugged. 'No knife was found in the cargo hold. We unloaded quite a pile of goods at the dock and took a second look.'

'Mort Lindsay is the man who searched for the knife right after the fight, Marshal,' Clay informed the lawman. 'I'd guess Lard's knife is presently under twenty feet of Colorado river water.'

Baxter shook his head. 'You got no one on your side here, Valenteen. Worse for you, both Lard and Mort work for Warren Locke, who is a close friend to Judge Stickley.'

Clay groaned. 'I can sure pick 'em.'

'There was a stowaway on board too,' Captain Mellon added. 'He was hiding in the cargo hold. I don't see how he could have missed the fight. Valenteen tripped him up when he tried to flee the scene.

'He as much as admitted he saw the fight to me, but he refused to speak up in front of the captain,' Clay related. 'He's a scared kid, but there's no doubt he saw Lard pull the knife and attack me.'

The marshal rested his haunch on the

18

corner of his desk. He was on the long side of forty, as crusty and hard as week-old bread. His eyes were clear with the insight of years, a thick handle-bar moustache was neatly trimmed beneath a prominent nose and several crooked teeth were visible when he spoke. Will Baxter had wide shoulders, a slight middle-age paunch, yet he appeared both capable and sturdy.

'What are you going to do with that stow-away, Captain?' he asked.

'Company has rules,' Mellon replied. 'The boy will have to make restitution and earn his fare. If we let one mother's son get away with stowing away, we would have a dozen wharf rats sneaking aboard every week.'

Tipping back his hat, the marshal scratched his shaggy head and put a curious look on Clay. 'You're dead certain the freeloader saw the ruckus betwixt you and Lard?'

Clay said, 'He couldn't have missed it, Marshal. The trouble is how to get him to speak up.'

'Be worth a heap if the boy was to confirm your story, I'd think.'

'That's true enough. What are you getting at?'

'If I recall, the fare from here to San Francisco is around ninety dollars. You carrying enough to square things with the captain?'

Clay reached inside his pocket and pulled out his traveling money. 'I've got ... seventy ... eighty-three dollars.'

Jack Mellon had picked up on the marshal's train of thought. 'I suppose we could give the kid a break on the full price, considering he didn't have either decent food or a place to sleep.'

'How much?' Baxter asked.

'Fifty dollars ought to square things.'

Baxter looked back at Clay. 'What do you say? If that kid don't speak up on your behalf, you might never have need of money again. Judge Stickley ain't one to crowd the jails.'

Clay put a hand to his throat, thinking of how uncomfortable it would feel to have a rope tightening around his neck. He counted out fifty dollars and handed it to the steamboat captain.

'Not a word about this to the stowaway,' Baxter pointed out to both men. 'Captain, you tell the boy he is being prosecuted and bring him in here. The thought of some jail time might throw enough of a scare into him to loosen his tongue.'

Jack grinned. 'I'll have him here in an hour.'

Baxter herded Clay towards a single cell. He spent a moment untying his hands, then locked him inside the small barred room.

'If you try and put any undue pressure on that stowaway, I'll figure you must've killed Lard Ackers in cold blood and let you face the judge alone. His death is no loss to society, but the law is the law.'

Clay gave a nod of understanding and laced his fingers around the cell bars. He watched, while the marshal went over to his desk and looked over the few things Clay had in his traveling bag. The lawman spent several long moments looking over the different items offered by the Original Grange Supply House.

'Growing bigger all the time. I remember just a year or two back that your company only had a single sheet of goods. Now they put out several pages and have some drawings too.' He showed a crooked grin, 'You got any of them listings that have pictures of women's corsets and the like?'

'In the bottom of the suitcase,' Clay told him. 'We have a couple pages especially for the ladies. I keep the merchandise separated in their own categories, so I can show a person what interests him most. If I handed over the ladies' pages along with the ones on blacksmith tools, timepieces and the like, no one would pay attention to what I wanted to sell them.'

Baxter dug down to the bottom of the bag, removed the pages and glanced over the drawings. 'Bust my buttons, sonny!' he exclaimed, eyeing the artwork, 'Do you think one day these lady's delicates might be photographed with real women doing the modeling? That would sure enough get some interest for your catalogs.'

'I wouldn't hold my breath,' Clay replied. 'What decent woman would ever pose in her unmentionables for the likes of a catalog?'

'None that I know of, but there are gals who pose for artists and such. It wouldn't be much of a jump to being in a photograph.'

'You could be right,' Clay allowed, 'but it would most likely have to be soiled doves, women without honor.'

Baxter displayed a wistful mien. 'I sometimes wonder what happened to the gal who has her painting on the wall behind the bar of the Lost Cache Saloon. She's a real beauty.'

'I haven't seen the inside of the saloon yet. I hope that, once this thing with Lard is settled, I get the chance.'

Baxter put back the catalog pages and laughed. 'Guess you do have other things to think about at that. Bet you wish you'd come up-river on a different steamboat.'

'Especially if Stickley hears my case. The captain says he a hard man.'

'He can be tough,' Baxter agreed. 'Both he and Locke arrived here shortly after the war ended between the Union and Confederacy. Locke owns a local mercantile store, plus a warehouse and saddle shop. His freight out-fit delivers goods and supplies to ranches and outlying villages, plus he has a few tough hands on his payroll ... including Lard Ackers and Mort Lindsay.'

'What about the judge himself?'

'He owns the hotel, but an elderly couple run it for him,' Baxter answered. 'There's a rumor he was in good with the last governor and the judgeship was repayment of sorts.'

'Is he an honest man?'

'He seems a fair-minded man who deals out justice with a heavy hand. As for his personal history, I don't know the details about how Stickley became a judge, but I know the few men he has sentenced to hang are all dead.'

Clay sat down on one of the two cots in the cell and grimaced. The mattress felt like two sheets of pasteboard stuck together, there was no pillow and only a solitary army blanket at the foot of each bunk. Sleep within the cell would be from necessity rather than comfort. The floor of the cell was hardpack earth, while the rear and side wall were constructed of mortared brick. The rest of the building was sod and wood, but the cell had been built to hold the most desperate of men.

'Maybe you'll get lucky?' the marshal said, taking note of Clay's dismay at being locked in a cell.

'How's that?'

'They have started work on a territorial prison here in Yuma. If the boy don't speak up on your behalf, you might be lucky enough to be sentenced right here to help build it.'

'Now there's a cheery thought.' Clay grunted cynically. 'A man wouldn't last a year busting rocks under the Arizona sun in the heat of summer.'

The marshal laughed and dug out a chaw of tobacco. He bit off a chunk, then chewed and rolled it about in his mouth. After a few passes, the chaw settled against his right cheek, forming a lump like a chipmunk with a mouthful of nuts.

A short while later a seaman arrived with the youngster in tow. He gave the kid a shove into the room and displayed a knowing smirk.

'Compliments of the captain,' he said. 'The young hellion be all yours, Marshal.'

Even under the mixture of dirt and grime from hiding aboard the steamship, the boy looked pale. Clay didn't doubt he had been sick on board ship. Any food he might have scrounged *en route*, before his capture, had likely been tainted or even spoiled. Plus, he wasn't much for size in the first place, maybe an inch over five-foot and a gaunt hundred pounds.

The marshal took custody of the young prisoner and escorted him to the cell.

'I suspect you know your bunkmate,' Baxter jeered.

The kid's eyes grew wide. As the marshal opened the door, his expression changed from dread to mortal terror.

'Now mind your manners,' he teased the lad. 'I don't want you pushing Valenteen around and bullying him.'

'No! You can't put me—' the youth began a panicked protest.

But Baxter pushed him through the opening and clanked the door closed. He watched with some amusement as the boy scampered off to a corner, getting as far away from Clay as possible.

'Marshal,' Clay complained, after a few

moments, 'gamy as I am from travel, it's obvious my new room-mate needs a bar of soap and a thorough scrubbing. How about allowing us the use of some water and a tub?'

'Good idea,' Baxter agreed. 'I have to live here, too, and my nose is already starting to twitch from the smell.'

Within minutes, Baxter provided a washtub, a drying cloth, soap, and then he added enough water to fill the tub about half full. When finished with the chore he winked at Clay.

'It's coming on to suppertime. Whilst the two of you do your personal laundry, I'll see if I can rustle up something to eat. If either of you need anything, let out a holler.'

The boy flew to the cell door. He pressed his face up against the bars, while his hands gripped the rounded bars until the whites of his knuckles showed.

'Please, Marshal Baxter,' he pleaded in a raspy voice. 'Please don't leave me in here with this man.'

'You mind your manners, sonny,' Baxter answered back, 'and Valenteen won't do you any harm.

'You don't understand!' he whimpered, ready to break down and cry.

Baxter waggled a finger to silence his protests, pivoted about wordlessly and went out the jailhouse door.

Clay waited until the marshal had left before turning his attention to the boy. The kid acted as if he had a raging fear of water. He took one frightened look at the tub and immediately curled up on one of the bunks. Burying his face behind his dirty hands, he cowered like a scolded pup, quivering from head to foot.

The marshal had provided Clay with his spare change of clothes from his traveling bag. For the stowaway, he had found a relatively clean pair of jeans and shirt. Clay didn't wish to wash in the dirt and grime the boy would leave behind him in the tub, so he stripped off his clothes and took the first wash. Once finished he donned his spare set of clothes and began to feel like a human being again.

'It's your turn, you grubby little beggar,' he spoke to the boy. 'Are you going to co-operate or do I have to strip you down and physically stick you in the washtub?'

Billy sprang up, sitting erect, his face a mask of terror. He gave a violent shake of his head and raised both hands, tightly balled into fists. 'You keep away from me!' he warned in a squeaking, high-pitched shriek.

'You touch me and I'll–'

Clay was in no mood for games. He had taken all he was going to take from the ragged, dirty, tight-lipped joker. His silence had caused Clay to be chained to a riverboat wall and thrown into a city jail. Added to that, he had forked out fifty dollars in cash to save the boy from a lot of trouble. He was through being gentle with the sniveling brat.

He crossed the distance between them in a single stride and reached for the boy. Billy swung at him with both hands, but the blows lacked any real punch or power. Clay deftly batted the kid's hands aside, grabbed a handful of his shirt and yanked him off of the bunk.

The boy instantly became more fierce and determined. He flailed away at Clay, swinging wildly, slapping and clawing at his arms. Clay was much stronger than the boy, but the small-framed youth kicked and squirmed like a spooked wildcat. When Clay pinned his wrists together in one hand, the battling youth lowered his head and bit him on the arm.

That was the final straw. Clay jerked Billy off his feet, whirled about and bodily slammed him down to the floor. The action knocked the wind from the boy's lungs. He lay there dazed, with his mouth wide open, gasping to catch his breath. Before he could regain his strength Clay pinned each of the boy's arms under a knee and sat down on his mid-section. With the youngster helpless to fight back, he gave a yank and tore open the front of the kid's shirt. The aggressive action sent a couple of buttons flying and caused a second immediate reaction – an ear-splitting scream!

Clay froze. The voice sounded like...

'Please!' the youth wailed. 'Stop!'

Clay's brain refused to decipher this new information leaving him momentarily dumbfounded.

Billy tossed his head back and forth until his floppy hat became dislodged. The negative motion also shook loose a shock of ginger-colored hair. When he lifted his head up from the floor, the hair unraveled to spill about the youth's shoulders, while a healthy dose of bangs showered down over Billy's red flushed face.

Aghast at the turn of events, Clay hastily released the shirt material and lifted his hands, palms outward, as if in a sign of surrender. He sat back and lifted his knees enough to allow Billy to remove his arms from where he'd had them pinned. Billy grabbed the shirt front and drew the two remnants tightly together.

'What the devil?' Clay exclaimed breathlessly. 'You're not a boy.'

'No, I'm not!' Billy blurted out the words. 'Curse your ornery hide! I'm a girl!'

CHAPTER TWO

Clay sprang to his feet as if he had been astraddle a hot stove! He stared in awe at the dirty, oval face, distorted at present by Billy's effort not to bawl. She didn't fully win the battle for composure as a couple of tears slid down her smudged cheeks.

'Please,' she murmured, rolling her head from side to side. 'Just let me alone.'

Clay gulped down his shock and recovered his senses. 'Not until you answer some questions, little britches.'

'I'm not answering anything!' she snapped, obviously angered and humiliated by the situation.

Clay had his own humiliation to think about. He had spent some time around different girls, even skinny-dipped with his two sisters as a little kid, but he'd never taken a bath in front of a strange woman.

'Why the lies?' he wanted to know. 'Why didn't you speak up for me? What's the idea of pretending to be a man?'

She didn't offer a reply.

Clay leaned over, took hold of her wrists and glared into her dirty, tear-streaked face. He allowed his annoyance and chagrin to infuse his tone, making it harsh and menacing.

'In about one minute, I'm going to help you remove those filthy clothes, put you into that tub of water and give you a good scrubbing – girl or not! You'd better do some fast talking to change my mind.'

The ominous vow caused her to gasp, 'You wouldn't!'

'Make up your mind, girl!' Clay hissed the words. 'You either answer my questions or I'll strip you down and scrub you like the spoiled brat you are!'

She blinked away the tears and rolled her head from side to side. However, when Clay let go of her wrists and reached to take hold of her shirt, it prompted an immediate response.

'Wait!' she cried. 'I'll tell you whatever you want to know!'

Clay straightened up and moved back a

31

step. The little beggar sat up, modestly holding her shirt together with one hand. Her body trembled from the tussle, as she got up off of the dirt floor and sat down on the edge of the bunk.

'You can talk while you wash,' Clay informed her tersely. 'I'll keep my back to you.'

She scoffed at the idea. 'I'm not going to take a bath with you in the room!'

Clay's patience had expired. He was tired of the foolish charade, tired of being held a prisoner and tired of being made a fool.

'No more idle threats, little britches,' he told her gravely. 'It's time for you to get yourself into that tub and remove those layers of dirt and grime. You can either trust me to keep my back turned, or I'll give you a helping hand!'

She sucked in her breath. 'But I'm a girl!'

'A girl who sat there and let me take a bath without a word of warning.'

'I didn't look,' she blurted out. 'I hid my eyes the whole time.'

'And I'll provide you the same courtesy,' Clay assured her. 'Now I'm going to start counting,' he vowed menacingly. 'If you aren't in the tub and scrubbing yourself by the time I reach *ten*, I'm going to help you get the job done.'

He locked eyes with the girl, displaying a grim determination. 'One ... two...'

Her hands flew to the suspenders which held up her pair of oversized trousers. She sniffed to stop another flow of tears, but Clay had convinced her he was not bluffing. He rotated around facing the office door and continued.

'Three ... four...' he went forward with the count. 'Five ... six ... seven...'

Before he reached eight there came the sound of water splashing out on to the floor.

'All right!' she wailed. 'I'm in! I'm in the tub!'

'I suggest you make it quick,' Clay suggested callously. 'Marshal Baxter could return at any minute and he might not be the gentleman I am.'

'Yeah,' the words grated between her teeth, 'you're a real *gentleman!*'

In spite of the desperate situation and facing possible murder charges, Clay grinned. A little payback felt pretty good.

Baxter stood at the cell door and stared dumbly at the girl. She sat on the edge of the cot with a blanket wrapped about her from her ankles to her neck.

'Jumpin' horny toads, Valenteen!' he

declared. 'I knowed water to do some strange things, but I never seen it turn a boy into a girl before.'

'Kind of surprised me too.'

Baxter laughed heartily. 'Wish I'd have stuck around. Bet you had your hands full getting her in the bath.'

'I got in the washtub on my own!' Billy informed him sharply.

The marshal's face skewed into a frown. 'I guess the clothes I set aside for him ... uh, *her* to wear ain't exactly proper attire for a girl. I'll see if I can round up a dress. Wouldn't want her offending the judge at the trial.'

Billy's face colored noticeably and Baxter asked, 'So what's your name, miss?'

'Billy Jo Haversack,' she replied softly.

'Where you from?'

'Down-river.

'And what are you doing here in Yuma?'

'Sitting in jail,' she answered drily.

He laughed and winked at Clay. 'Cute as a mouse's ear, ain't she?'

'She claims she dressed as a boy to keep from getting harassed. A girl traveling alone might have drawn the wrong kind of attention.'

'So you run away from home?' Baxter prodded her.

She ignored the question.

Clay gave her a nudge. 'You're going to do real well on that steamboat, working off the ninety-dollar fare. Bet you are the most popular deck hand they ever had.'

Billy Jo's lips pressed together, forming a tight line.

'Like as not, she won't get a minute's peace,' Baxter continued the verbal assault. 'Wouldn't want to change places with her – especially at night.'

'I don't see what choice she has,' Clay said. 'I recall the captain saying a stowaway had to work off his debt. A couple of weeks from today and she'll be right back where she started from.'

The conversation had an effect. A mixture of uncertainty and dread entered the girl's make-up. She pretended to be as tough as a seasoned wrangler, but she suffered from the same vulnerability and fears as most other people.

'Maybe there's a way the gal can get around the captain's threat,' Baxter said, watching the bait squirm on the hook. 'If she was to tell what she seen the night you and Lard went at it, that might set real good with the judge.'

Billy Jo regarded them warily. She glanced from one man to the other and nervously licked her lips. 'You mean he might let me go? Just for telling the truth about the fight?'

'I reckon it would be a step in the right direction,' Baxter told her. 'We ain't got much need for female prisoners in Yuma, and I'll wager Captain Mellon don't want the trouble of a young, single female on his boat.'

Billy Jo took a deep breath and let it out slowly. 'I saw the fight,' she admitted at last. 'Mr Valenteen told it straight. The other man pulled a knife and attacked him.'

'That sounds more like the Lard Ackers I knew.' Baxter grunted. 'Kind of wish I had been there when he was planted in the ground – would have enjoyed spitting on his grave.'

'Why didn't you tell Captain Mellon the truth to start with?' Clay asked her.

'His friend – that Mort fellow – he told me to keep my mouth shut, or he'd hurt me. He was free and you were already bound up for murder.' She shrugged her slight shoulders. 'I didn't want to risk being found out or have my throat cut.'

'Will you repeat what you just said in front of the judge?' Baxter wanted to know.

She sighed resignedly. 'Yes, I'll tell him the truth.'

'Now that you're in Yuma,' Baxter changed

the subject, 'What did you have in mind for your next move? Were you going to continue to pretend to be a man and join the army to fight the Indians or something?'

'Of course not,' she answered.

'So why did you come all the way to Yuma?'

'I came here to find someone,' she admitted. 'Once I locate him, I won't trouble you again.'

The marshal rubbed his chin. 'I know about every *hombre* in these parts. Who is it you're lookin' for?'

A spark of interest entered her eyes. 'His name is Flint Cooner.'

Baxter snorted in disgust. 'What on earth do you want with a man like Flint?'

She frowned. 'That's between him and me.'

'You know him, Marshal?' Clay asked, wondering at Baxter's negative reaction.

'Yeah, I know him. He works for Locke too.'

'Sonuvabee!' Clay exclaimed. 'Does everyone in Yuma work for this guy Locke?'

'He does have his hand in a number of different pies. Matter of fact, he pays a sizeable portion of the taxes that pay my wages each month.'

'Did you send word to this Flint character that you were coming?' Clay asked the girl.

She shook her head, the wet strands of hair moving along her shoulders with the motion.

'You're not a sixteen-year-old boy,' Clay stated the obvious, 'so just how old are you, little britches?'

She glared at Valenteen. 'I told you my name is Billy Jo.'

'I'm curious too,' the marshal said. 'How old are you?'

'I'm old enough.'

Clay ventured, 'I'd wager she exaggerated about being sixteen.'

'My guess too,' Baxter agreed. 'More likely fourteen or thereabouts.'

'I turned eighteen last month!' she fired the words at them. 'I'm not a child!'

'Don't look that old,' Baxter observed.

'You want to count my teeth?' she cried. 'You'd do that with a horse!'

Clay chuckled at her outburst. 'Maybe she is telling the truth, Marshal. She's beginning to sound like a full-fledged woman.'

'Got the temper of one,' Baxter said with a grin. 'Wonder how Flint got mixed up with the likes of her?'

'If you don't mind' – Billy Jo was growing angry – 'I haven't got any clothes on and I haven't eaten yet today. Do you intend to keep me wrapped in a blanket and starve

38

me, or what?'

Baxter looked at the loaf of bread in his hand. 'I'll check around and see if I can find you something to wear. As for a meal, I was going to give you each a couple slices of bread to hold you over until breakfast. I expect I can do a little better than that for a young lady.'

Clay glanced at the girl and winked. 'See how much better treatment you get as a girl, little britches? He was going to give us a hunk of dry bread to eat. With you being such a proper lady and all, he is probably going to break out his mother's finest table setting.'

'Why don't you untangle your coils and slither away,' she retorted. 'I said I'd save your snake skin when we talk to the judge. What more do you want?'

'Maybe I can return the favor.'

'The only thing I want from you is to be left alone. As soon as I get some clothes and put something in my stomach, I intend to catch up on my sleep.'

'Sounds like good advice.'

'So quit looking at me.'

'It's a natural curiosity, little britches,' he excused his lack of manners. 'I was trying to think how you'd look in a dress, with your hair combed and a coy smile on your face.'

She frowned. 'You were easier to be around when you thought I was a man.'

'Correction, little britches,' he laughed at her statement. 'I thought you were a boy, but I never mistook you for a man.'

The remark increased the flood of anger to her features, but Clay only smiled a bit wider.

Delbert Stickley wore the faded black robe of a judge. His eyes were steel-gray, overshadowed by dark, bushy eyebrows. There was a sprinkle of gray above his ears and his hair had receded until the top of his head resembled a smooth, polished rock protruding above the grass line in an open meadow. He regarded Clay with a stern look while he listened to Billy Jo give her testimony. Once she had finished, he rolled an unlit cigar from one corner of his mouth to the other and beheld her with a steady gaze.

'The court thanks you for coming forward, young lady.' He said the right words, but there was no gratitude in his demeanor. When he swung his stare back to Clay, he did so with unveiled suspicion.

'It's real convenient, Mr Valenteen, having this young stowaway back up your story about Lard pulling a knife.' He grunted sarcastically. 'Strange that no knife was found at the scene of the fight.'

'I believe Mort Lindsay tossed the knife into the river, Your Honor,' Clay replied. 'Maybe he wanted to see if it could swim.'

The judge continued to scowl. 'This court has no problem with a self-defense plea, but I have pause to wonder if your paying the young woman's fare for the riverboat travel had anything to do with her sudden change of memory?'

Billy Jo cast a sharp glance at Clay and yelped, 'You did what?'

'We didn't say anything to the girl about the arrangement with the steamship captain,' the marshal spoke up on Clay's behalf. 'I only told her that speaking the truth might help her cause. I believe she told it straight about what happened. This fellow killed Lard in self-defense.'

The judge accepted the marshal's explanation but was not completely satisfied. 'I'm still curious as to why Lard Ackers would attack you, Mr Valenteen. If you are, as you claim, only a sales representative for the Grange Supply House, why would he try to kill you?'

'Beats me, Judge,' Clay replied innocently. 'I told him I was trying to locate my luggage, but he wouldn't listen. I can tell you one thing certain, no man in his right mind would have gone looking for a fight with a man the size of Lard Ackers.'

Stickley considered the words, while continuing to regard Clay with a narrow scrutiny. He chewed on the end of his cigar and finally gave his head a distinct nod.

'This court accepts the evidence as presented to be factual,' he stated professionally. 'As for you, Mr Valenteen, it might be wise if you were to finish your business in Yuma and be on your way. Lard had some friends here who might take exception to you taking his life.'

'Yes, sir, Your Honor.'

'Given the testimony of the only witness, the ruling is self-defense.' The judge banged his gavel. 'This hearing is adjourned.'

Clay let out the breath he'd been holding for several days. He was a free man once more and it was a great relief. He would have been in a major mess if he had been found guilty. He turned to leave, but Billy Jo stepped over to block his path.

'Mr Valenteen,' she said passionately, 'I will pay you back every cent you have spent on my behalf. I refuse to be in your debt.' She floundered momentarily. 'I ... I don't have any money right now, but you will get every penny.'

Clay dismissed her concern. 'You see to your own welfare first, little britches. Once you get settled, we can discuss arrangement for payment.'

She nodded her assent and left the small courtroom. As she walked away, Clay noticed she appeared much older and more mature than when she had pretended to be a boy. Her tawny hair had been brushed out and pulled back into a ponytail. It was held in place with the faded orange ribbon Baxter had provided, along with the modest, well-worn yellow dress she was wearing.

'Makes a right pretty gal, don't she?' Baxter asked Clay, having moved over to stand at his side.

'I'm a might perplexed at how I ever thought that little gal was a boy,' Clay replied. 'Who would have thought a little dirt and men's baggy clothes could hide that much of a young woman?'

'Judge Stickley was being polite when he said you aren't exactly welcome here in Yuma. I'd move on right sudden, if I was you.'

'Soon as I fill enough orders to earn the money for another ticket, Marshal. This episode on the riverboat cost me most of my traveling money.'

'Maybe you could send a wire and get some credit at the bank.'

Clay looked at the marshal. 'You trying to get rid of me?'

'Warren Locke isn't going to be real keen about having one of his men killed. His other hounds, Bung Tarkington, Mort Lindsay or even Flint Cooner is liable to try and even the score for Lard. You'd best watch your step.'

'If trouble comes, it won't be from my starting it. I only want to finish my job and head for cooler country. This heat is more than I'm used to.'

'Where do you hail from?'

'Mostly back East until the last year or two. These past few months I've been working out of Denver, Colorado. I'm not used to this hot climate of yours.'

'You came at the wrong time of year, Valenteen. When winter rolls around, this is the place to be. It stays nice and warm and we don't see that white stuff on the ground here.'

'If I ever have occasion to return to Yuma, I'll keep that in mind.'

Baxter lifted a hand in parting. 'Be seeing you, Valenteen. Stay out of trouble.'

'That's always my intention, Marshal.'

Billy Jo walked the length of the main street, before stopping to inquire about Flint Cooner at the bakery. The couple running the place were helpful, but seemed curiously dismayed by her inquiry.

Their opinion of Flint made no difference to Billy Jo. She had been trapped and helpless back home. Running away had been the only escape open to her. Flint had offered her a way out and she had jumped at the chance.

Following the directions she'd gotten at the bakery, she went down a side street to a row of adobe huts. The fourth shanty on the left was where she would find Flint. She hurried her step, anxious to feel the strength and comfort of being in the man's arms. He might even have enough money to pay back Valenteen. She wanted to be rid of that debt. The man had humiliated her while locked in the jail cell and made her feel cheap and foolish. If she never set eyes on that man again, it would be the greatest blessing of her life.

As she approached, she hoped Flint was home. He had bragged about earning big money, but the hut didn't reflect any great amount of wealth. One dirty window, a weathered and splintery door, with a sagging roof and single chimney. From its small dimensions Billy Jo surmised it could be no larger than two rooms. It made no difference at this point; there was no turning back.

Billy Jo inhaled to bolster her courage, walked up to the door and put her knuckles to it. She heard a soft stirring inside and summoned a smile to her lips as the door opened.

To her utter shock, a woman stood framed in the doorway. Though it was nearly noon, the lady wore only a thin robe over a dark red chemise and rather sheer black stockings. She was probably twice Billy Jo's age, with hard lines etched into her face and at the corners of her squinting black eyes. Straw-like, unkempt hair was assembled atop her head like a dirty yellow mop too long unrinsed, while her darkly painted lips puckered with disdain.

'What'cha want, squirt?' she asked sourly.

'I – I must have the wrong house,' Billy Jo stammered. 'I was looking for Mr Cooner.'

'Who is it, Lotty sweetness?' Flint's familiar voice came from inside the hut.

The woman grunted in disgust and turned her head to speak over her shoulder. 'It's another of those daffy, wide-eyed farm girls. Damn your lecherous hide, Flint. Do you have to give every huckleberry farm hick you meet the come-on?'

Billy Jo took a step back, her mind reeling.

She'd traveled all the way from California to be with Flint. She had endured insufferable heat, terrible food, tepid drinking water and the mortification of pretending to be a man. He'd made her big promises and told her he loved her. She had even allowed him to kiss her – twice!

Flint appeared behind the woman. He wore no shirt, revealing a soft ripple of fat about his belly that she had not detected during their previous brief encounters. In his hand, he carried a half-empty bottle of whiskey. It was mid-morning yet he appeared half drunk. He stared dumbly at Billy Jo and a glimmer of recognition slowly entered his red-rimmed eyes.

'Well, I'll be the son of a monkey's uncle! It's Billy Jo ... uh.' He obviously didn't remember her last name. 'Hey, honeycomb! This is a real surprise!' He smiled and pulled on the half-clad woman's arm. 'Let me have a few words with her, Lotty sweetness.'

Lotty snorted contemptuously. 'Just don't be bringing her into the house. I ain't running no nursery for witless, runaway brats.'

Billy Jo couldn't get her brain to function. She stood rooted to the ground, staggered by the stark realization of how she had been a complete fool. It took the breath out of her lungs and caused a weakening of her legs. She ducked her head to conceal the flood of shame and regret that washed over her.

Flint stepped out of the house, closed the door and took up a position in front of her. He made a half-hearted effort to keep the bottle behind his back.

'I never expected to see you in Yuma, honeycomb.' He instilled the silky smoothness in his voice she remembered from their clandestine meetings. 'How did you get way up here?'

She mentally cursed herself for being so naïve. His gentle tone and tender words had sounded so inviting and romantic to her ears. How many other girls had he coerced with his dastardly beguilement?

'I – I came by riverboat,' she mumbled awkwardly. 'I thought...' A sob of humiliation caused her voice to crack. She angrily swallowed the lump in her throat and blurted out, 'You said you loved me and wanted to marry me!'

Flint reached for her, but Billy Jo backed up a step to keep her distance. She was not going to allow the lying cheat to ever touch her again – not ever!

'Billy, Billy,' Flint whispered softly. 'I didn't expect you to come all this way. I was only having a little fun with you. I didn't expect you to take a coupla harmless kisses seriously.'

'A kiss is supposed to be sacred!' she fired back at him.

'Damn, girl,' he said gently, 'you're not much more than a kid. I'm at least twice your age. There could never be anything permanent betwixt us.'

Billy Jo had no reply. She had seen Flint's proposal as an escape route, a chance to be free and escape the nightmare of her life. Being so anxious to get away, she had been willing to run away with the first man who asked. Seeing Flint now, half drunk, his beer belly covering his belt, with a painted, acid-tongued woman in his house, she couldn't believe she'd been quite that desperate.

'I'm sorry if I caused you any trouble,' she finally managed to speak again.

'Lotty is used to it,' Flint was off-hand about it. 'It isn't often such a pretty girl shows up on my doorstep, but there have been others.'

Her anger consumed her humiliation. 'You must be very proud of yourself, telling your lies to innocent girls all over the country.'

'What's the harm?' he chided her. 'So I kissed you a coupla times, so what? A girl has to grow up sometime.'

Billy Jo wished she had the courage to slap the man's leering face. Instead, she spun on her heels and stormed away.

'Come back when you're a little older,' Flint's voice followed after her. 'Lotty isn't getting any younger.'

Neither are you! she wanted to shout back. But the sob lodged in her throat prevented any reply. She ran down the street blindly and sought sanctuary in a deserted alley. Once alone and out of sight, she leaned up against the building and cried the tears out of her system. The weeping was not from sorrow or disappointment, but out of frustration. She had worked so hard to get this far, sacrificed her dignity and survived like a thief and beggar. It had all been for nothing.

Billy Jo recuperated after a few minutes and got her thinking process working once more. She was in a strange town, penniless, without a friend in the world. She needed to find a job and a place to stay. She struggled to recover the tattered shreds of her dignity and set her sights on the days ahead. One thing she knew for certain, she would never accept the fate awaiting her back home. She would die first!

Darkness covered the sprawling town of Yuma like a thick, warm blanket. Even without the sun, heat radiated from the parched earth and the temperature remained near a hundred degrees.

Clay left the café, after having eaten a late meal, and walked down the street to the saloon. He hung around for a time, sipping a warm beer and watching for his contact. The man didn't show, but that wasn't unusual. The last time he had worked with Grady, they had not spoken a dozen words in the nearly two months it had taken to complete the assignment. Each of them knew their job and it was difficult and dangerous to cross paths too often. Clay decided he was wasting his time and left the saloon.

He had rented himself a room for a few days and would spend much of his time circulating his catalog to the townsfolk and nearby ranches or farms. His goal was to bring in enough orders to justify his cover. The earnings from those sales were of little consequence. His real task still lay ahead of him.

He greeted the desk clerk and asked for some matches. It would insure the man remembered him coming in. When he had signed for the room earlier, the person

51

behind the counter had been a short, rather plain woman. He recalled Baxter telling him the judge owned the hotel. This then was the other half of the married couple whom he had running the place.

The room was suited to his needs, as it was at the back of the building and on the ground floor. Once inside, he sank down on the bed for a few minutes and then put out his lamp. To anyone paying attention, it would appear that he had gone to bed for the night.

Clay waited a bit before moving to the window. Hidden within the darkness, he pulled aside the edge of the curtain and looked out to the main avenue. After a careful search, he spied a shadowy figure in the alleyway across the street. As he suspected, his room was being watched. Killing Lard had been a necessity, but it raised suspicions about his purpose. Either someone wanted to keep an eye on him personally, or they took a special interest in every newcomer.

Clay considered his situation. The marshal seemed an honest sort and the judge was gruff, but he had been fair. He had not met Warren Locke as yet, the man to whom the rifles were consigned as 'farm tools', so he had not formed an opinion about him. If he turned out to be the man Clay was after, the situation could prove as difficult as trying to drink from a beer mug while on the back of a bucking bronco. Locke had money, power, several hired guns on his payroll and was friends with Judge Stickley. Those were formidable odds to tackle before Clay had even conferred with his partner.

Five minutes passed and the man tossed away the cigarette he'd been smoking. As he came into the light from a shop window, Clay perceived the watcher to be a slender man, taller than most, with a flat-crowned hat and a gun on either hip. It was too dark to make out his face but Clay would keep an eye out for anyone wearing two guns.

Once the man disappeared down the street, Clay eased out the window and slipped silently along the side of the building. After taking a careful look around, he crossed to the shadows on the opposite side of the street.

During the day, he had memorized the streets and alleyways. He went down a passage and padded softly behind the Lost Cache Saloon. It was the biggest place in that part of town, except for a couple of warehouses that were located down by the livery.

Clay moved with stealth, hiding his movements within the shadows. He remained vigilant as he trotted up to the rear entrance of the general store. From the vantage point he could see the Locke warehouse. It was not as large as a barn, but there would be room enough inside to stockpile several wagonloads of merchandise. He started moving forward, thinking he would slip over to the building and maybe get a look inside, but his luck ended at that moment. There was a night guard on duty.

Clay darted quickly into the livery barn for cover, before the sentry spotted him. Lost within the darkness, he could hear animals moving out back and the stale smell of straw and horse leavings assailed his nostrils.

He stood for a moment, allowing his eyes to adjust to the dark, sorting through his limited options. There was no way to enter the small warehouse without alerting the guard. So long as the man remained on duty, Clay would be unable to get inside and check for the crates which had been in the cargo hold of the riverboat. As he had not been in contact with Grady, he didn't know if his time in jail had cost him the purpose of their mission. He studied on an idea to get the guard to leave his post. With him out of the way, he could do the neces-sary snooping in a matter of minutes. He needed a diversion of some kind.

Even as he mulled over ideas, something moved from within the darkness, a shadowy figure streaked toward him and the open barn door. In the pitch black of the stable, he couldn't see if the phantom had a weapon. Instinctively, he stooped low and threw his body in front of him.

His unexpected action took the legs out from under the ghostly figure and brought him down onto his hands and knees. Before he could react, Clay jumped on his back, using his weight to drive the man to the ground. The phantom grunted from the weight and swore.

'What the Sam Hill is your problem?'

Clay realized the body beneath him was not the man who had been keeping tabs on him. It was much worse – the culprit was wearing a dress: he had tackled a woman!

Hastily, he clamped a hand over the woman's mouth so she wouldn't scream–

The female bit into the fleshy part of his hand. He cursed under his breath and jerked back from the bite. The gal rolled over, bucking like a spooked bronc and flailing at him with two flying fists.

Smacks and slaps scored hits about Clay's head and chest until he caught hold of the woman's wrists and pinned her beneath his own weight.

'Hold on! Take it easy!' he coaxed softly. 'I'm not going to hurt you. Be still!'

The woman stopped her struggle, her chest heaving mightily from the exertion. After several seconds, the lady complained.

'Are you going to let me up?'

'I thought you were going to attack me,' Valenteen explained hurriedly. 'I didn't know you were a woman.'

'I'm getting real tired of you sitting on my middle, Valenteen!'

He now recognized the voice. 'Little britches?'

'For a salesman, you sure do a lot of snooping,' she said in a constrained tone. 'What are you doing sneaking around in the stable?'

He removed his weight from the girl, knelt on the ground next and fingered a tender spot on his cheek where she had struck him.

'What are you doing in here?' he queried.

'I asked you first,' she shot back, rising to a sitting position. 'And why are you always sneaking around in dark places, attacking anyone you come across?'

Clay stood up and helped the girl to her feet. There was enough light from the moon streaming through the open door of the stable for Clay to see the outline of Billy Jo Haversack. She ran her fingers through her hair to remove several strands of straw, then brushed off her dress. He could see she was wearing an old, ragged coat. It carried an odor of something which had been dug out of someone's trash.

'What happened to your friend Flint?' He ignored her own questions.

'That's none of your business.'

He gave a negative shake of his head. 'Picked yourself a real gentleman, didn't you?' He did not mask the sarcasm. 'Good of him to put you up for the night where you can share a stable with the horses.'

'Horses are better company than most of the men I've known in my life,' she snapped back.

Clay glanced across the yard at the man guarding the small warehouse, before returning his attention to the girl.

'How'd you like to sleep in a real bed tonight?'

'You making some kind of indecent pro-position?' Her voice held a tight warning. ''Cause, if you are, I'll sure enough stick you with a pitchfork in a place where you won't like it.'

'Take it easy, little britches,' he told her

passively. 'This is on the level.'

Her tone was mocking. 'Sure it is.'

'Listen, if you give me a hand, you can have my room at the hotel.'

'And what about you?'

'I won't be needing a room tonight.'

'Why should I help you?'

'You'd be helping yourself,' he countered. 'It's obvious your pal Flint didn't take care of you. You need a place to stay and I need a diversion for that guard over there.'

There was enough moonlight seeping into the barn that he saw Billy Jo frown. She stared over at the guard sitting next to the warehouse door. When she turned back towards Clay, he didn't have to see her face clearly to know there was mistrust in her eyes.

'Who are you?' she wanted to know. 'And why do you want to break into that storehouse?'

'Maybe I'm only curious.'

'I don't think so. You were snooping around on the boat when you were caught by that fellow you killed. You act like either a thief or some kind of lawman.'

'If I were a thief I wouldn't ask for your help; you could identify me to the marshal. And if I were a lawman I'd get the marshal's help to see what is in the back of that store-room.'

'So what are you looking for?'

'That's my business.' He avoided giving her an answer. 'Do you want the room or not?'

The girl thought for a moment, then said, 'What do I have to do?'

'Coax that man away from the door of the building. You only have to keep him busy for a few minutes.'

'A few minutes is asking a lot.'

'The window of my room is open. It's the last one at the rear of the building, in the alley next to the bakery. You only have to climb through to have a clean bed for the night. I'll even throw in breakfast for you.'

Billy Jo sighed. 'A real bed sounds good and all, but...' She hesitated. 'I'm not going to flirt with a strange man so what do I say to the guard?'

'First off, get rid of that smelly coat. Tell the guard you took a walk, or were with a friend, and you need to get back to your hotel. With the rowdies and drunks coming and going from the saloons, you would like for someone trustworthy to escort you back. If he will walk you as far as the hotel, I should have the time I need.'

The girl shrugged out of the coat and tossed it aside. 'This is only for one night,' she defended her decision. 'Once I get paid, I'll get a room of my own.'

'You found a job?'

'Yes, Mr Valenteen. I start work tomorrow morning. I'll expect that breakfast early.'

'Whenever you want,' he agreed.

Billy Jo took a deep breath. 'If I end up in jail again because of this, I'll need no prodding to spill the beans about you. I won't sit in a lousy cell on your account.'

'It won't come to that, little britches. Even if I were to be caught, no one would suspect an innocent child like you of helping me.'

'I'm not a child!' she flared.

He grinned at her spunk. 'So use your feminine wiles and get rid of that guard for me.'

'My what?'

'Just try to look helpless,' he told her, moving over to keep watch by the door. 'Most men respond to a lady in distress.'

The young woman left the stable and made a wide circle. Doing so made it appear she had come from the main street. Clay watched as she wandered along the back street. When she reached the guard the two of them began to speak.

Clay began to have second thoughts. What if the girl turned against him? What if the two of them left, only to return with a dozen armed men? What if she told the guard of his plan? Billy Jo might decide there was easy money to be made by informing on him. He dismissed the concern. Something told him he could trust her.

After a short exchange of conversation the sentry left his post. The man was cavalier enough not to allow a young lady to walk the streets alone at night. He tucked a shot-gun under one arm and they started up the street together.

Clay moved as soon as their backs were to him. It was only a short way to the hotel and the girl didn't exactly have a gift of gab. He couldn't hope she would entertain him for more than a couple of minutes. Using a special skeleton key and his knife to quickly open the door, he entered the storage ware-house. He found and inspected the crates, discovered what he wanted and quickly made his exit. He swiftly locked the door and padded around to the dark side of the building. Hugging the shadows, he made it safely to the barn moments before the guard returned to his post. The plan had worked.

CHAPTER THREE

Clay spent the night in the livery hay loft and left at sun-up, before the hostler was up and about. There was no clerk at the hotel reception desk so he made his way to his room without being observed. The bed showed use, but Billy Jo had not waited to take advantage of his offer of breakfast.

Eyes red and burning for lack of adequate sleep, Clay flopped down on the bed and caught a couple hours of sack time. He was up before noon, ate a late breakfast, then spent some time making sales pitches near the storehouse. He kept watch until mid-afternoon, but no wagons arrived or left for deliveries.

Clay decided to spend a little time at the saloon again. He didn't feel the need for a beer so early in the day, but casinos were a good place for gossip and picking up information. He stepped inside the batwing doors of the Lost Cache Saloon and spied Billy Jo.

She was in one corner of the room, sitting

behind a table, which was covered with a row of pastries. There were different cookies, rolls and several small spice cakes spread out in front of her. Two men were discussing the prices of the goods, joking and flirting with her at the same time.

Clay did an about-face and went down the street to the marshal's office. A few minutes later, he was back at the saloon with Baxter. Three young cowboys were at Billy Jo's table when they arrived. As the marshal approached, the trio quickly lost interest in the pastries and moved off toward the bar.

'I'll have to ask you to pack up your goods, Miss Haversack,' Marshal Baxter said gently. 'You can't be working in a place like this.'

Billy Jo fixed a stormy glare on Clay and jumped to her feet. 'I've heard tell a lot of saloons allow bakery goods to be sold in them. Since when is this crummy town any different!'

'Since you aren't old enough to be in here,' he replied evenly. 'No one is allowed in these places unless they are of legal age. For a woman, that's twenty-one years old!'

'But I'm not drinking or–'

The marshal held up his hand to stop her protest. 'Don't waste your breath, young lady. Pack up your pastries or I'll have to take you before the judge. He would sure enough fine you for being in a casino.'

'You did this!' she shouted at Clay, scorching him with smoldering hot eyes. 'You put the marshal on my back!'

'I'm only a law-abiding citizen,' he said inoffensively. 'I didn't want you getting into trouble.'

'Trouble!' she cried. 'All I've had since I met you is trouble!'

'Let's go,' the marshal said quietly. 'I'll help you carry the stuff back to Dick and Wilma at the bakery. I know they'll understand.'

It took all three of them to carry the special merchandise back to the bakery. While the marshal explained to the Jenkinses that Billy Jo couldn't work in the saloon, Clay started for the door. He was a little too slow. Billy Jo cornered him before he could get out of the shop.

'You've got a lot of nerve,' she bit off the heated words, her face flushed with anger, 'after what I did for you!'

'A saloon is no place for a decent young lady.'

'That's rich!' she said cynically, while mindful to keep her voice down. 'You get me to talk that guard off of his doorstep like a dancehall gal and now you claim I'm too decent to sell baked goods in a saloon!'

'Saloons can be dangerous. I didn't want to see you get hurt.'

'But you didn't mind seeing me lose my job, did you?'

Clay wondered how someone so small could throw around so much weight. Billy Jo pressed right against him, standing on her toes, glowering up at him. When this little lady got her dander up, she was fearsome enough to tackle a full grown grizzly.

'There are other places to sell baked goods. I'm sure the Jenkinses didn't think of the possible consequences of you working in a saloon.'

'Do me a favor, Mr Salesman,' Billy Jo hissed the words. 'From now on, stay out of my way and out of my life!'

The marshal had finished with talking to the Jenkinses and walked over to Clay. He overheard Billy Jo's farewell words and a wry grin spread across his face.

'Let's get out of here, Valenteen,' he said, holding back laughter. 'I'd hate to see that little gal lose her temper and beat you like a scrambled egg.'

'Right you are, Marshal. Lead the way.'

They followed Billy Jo out to the street, closing the door to the bakery behind them.

The girl stormed up the street and they were left standing on the walk.

'Old man Jenkins said it was the young girl's idea to set up shop in the saloon,' Baxter told Clay. 'She was going to work for what she could sell on her own. You know ... a commission job?'

'That's the way I work, Marshal. I get a commission on every order I take for the Grange Supply House.'

'You didn't make any points with that little fireball. She knows you came and got me.'

Clay uttered a sigh. 'We don't seem to be hitting it off very well at that.'

'You think she managed to find Flint?' Baxter wondered.

'I brought it up with her and she changed the subject. I'd guess she found him and learned that he was a lying, good-for-nothing, smooth-talking snake.'

'That's a proper description, Valenteen. Flint hangs his hat at a run-down shack a few blocks from here. The woman who owns the shanty is Lotty Dorf. She works dealing Faro at the Lost Cache. Good thing she didn't come on duty while your young friend was in there. Lotty is as mean and tough as a wild boar. If we had been going in to stop her from selling goods, I'd have wanted a dozen deputies backing me up.'

'I hope little britches steers clear of her.'

'For her sake, I hope so too.'

'Thanks for your help, Marshal. I didn't want to see the gal get off on the wrong foot.'

'I'll second the motion there.' He tipped his hat back enough to scratch his head. 'You ever find out where she came from?'

Clay lifted a shoulder in a shrug. 'She refuses to say a thing about it. Even on the boat, facing the charge of being a stowaway, she was as tight-lipped as a clam.'

'You making any sales?' Baxter changed the subject.

'Here and there. We're offering the Classic Peacemaker Colt .45 for seventeen dollars. That's a pretty good buy on a fine handgun.'

'The one with the regular seven-inch barrel?'

'That's right. But we also have the Sheriff's Model or the short-barrel gun for about the same price. You might like the four and three-quarter inch barrel. Be a lot quicker to get out of a holster.'

Baxter laughed. 'Comes to a quick draw in a fight, I'd do better to say a prayer instead. If I'm expecting trouble, I carry a shotgun. Wearing this badge, I don't have to prove I'm faster with a gun than some drunk.'

'No one with any brains tries to prove he's quicker on the trigger than someone else. I can't think of a more senseless thing to die over.'

'Well, you stay clear of Bung Tarkington or he'll be looking to try you on for size.'

'Bung?' Clay recalled the name. 'He wear two guns?'

Baxter's eyebrows closed together. 'You've already met him?'

'No, but I caught sight of a man keeping an eye on me last night. He had a gun on either hip.'

'That was probably Bung all right. He wears a matched set of walnut-handled Remington Frontier .44s. Let me tell you, Valenteen, he knows how to get those shootin' irons out of their holsters real sudden. I watched him practice one day.'

'I'll walk a wide circle around the man,' Clay promised.

The marshal laughed. 'You'd better give Billy Jo a wide berth too. She doesn't seem like the forgiving sort.'

'I believe you're right, Marshal. That girl has the temper of a wasp-stung mule.'

'Be seeing you, Valenteen.' He started to depart but added, 'Best put a rush on drumming up sales and finish up around town.

68

The heat you've been complaining about in Yuma ain't nothing to the heat you might feel, should you cross Bung or that girl again.'

'Thanks, Marshal. I'll watch out for them both.'

Warren Locke stood at the window of his office, which was directly above the general store. His hands were locked behind his back, as he watched the marshal and Clay Valenteen on the street below.

'See that?' he said over his shoulder. 'Valenteen keeps looking to see if there is anything going on over at the storehouse.'

Bung moved over to stand at the man's side. 'He's probably just a nosy sort. From what I've seen, the man is as curious as a cat. He's a salesman, Locke. His type is always looking for an angle to sell something to a customer.'

'I don't like him sniffing around.'

'You think Lard and Valenteen got into it because he caught the drummer looking though our crates?'

Locke sighed. 'I don't know. The girl backed up his story and Mort admitted some of Valenteen's belongings were in the hold. It could have all been a mistake on Lard's part, but the man strikes me as a little too worldly to be a simple salesman.'

'There might be a way to find out,' Bung offered.

'We need to be careful, Bung. This is a touchy time. I was having a drink with the judge the other day and he told me there was a rumor over at the governor's office that there's some sort of investigation going on down this way. He didn't know what kind of investigation exactly, but the news is enough for us to stay alert.'

'The governor don't know nothing about our operation.'

'That's why we have to be careful. If we were to kill a salesman for snooping around, it would alert every law dog in the country.'

'What I have in mind wouldn't cause any fuss.'

Locke rotated to look at his hired man. 'I'm listening.'

'You know the stowaway gal, the one who spoke up before the judge and supported Valenteen's claim of self-defense?'

'What about her?'

'Maybe she saw more than she told about Lard's death,' Bung suggested. 'I'd wager she knows if the man was looking for his baggage or if he was prying open boxes.'

'And why would she tell us?'

'She came to see Flint,' Bung explained. 'You know how that dog-in-heat mongrel tries to bed every naïve girl he comes across. He's the reason the girl made the trip to Yuma. She thought he wanted to marry her.'

Locke grunted in disgust. 'That man's got the morals of an alley cat. I'm glad I never married. I wouldn't trust that coyote around my wife for one minute.'

'True, but his wandering ways might help us this time. He could pay a visit to the little stowaway. Some well-chosen questions from him might just get us the answers we need.'

Lock nodded his agreement, while he continued to watch Valenteen's movements down on the street.

'Have a talk with Flint. I want answers by tonight. We can't be worrying about some snoop, when we are about to set a date for moving those rifles. If Valenteen isn't who and what he claims, he is going to have a fatal accident.'

Bung chuckled. 'Yuma can be a wild town; a lot of bad things can happen to a man. Besides which, if he should decide to ride out alone, there are a number of renegades roaming about. Man could end up dead and scalped real easy.'

'Let's see what we can find out first. Have

Flint talk to the girl, while I try and check the man out through other channels. No need to kill a completely innocent man.'

Bung grunted, 'I've never met a man who is completely innocent, Locke.'

'Get going, Bung. Time's a'wasting.'

'Oh,' Bung said, before leaving, 'there's a teamster outside waiting to see you about a job. He came up on the same steamship with Valenteen.'

'Send him in as you leave.'

The gunman left the room. A minute later a stranger entered. He wore work clothes, scuffed boots and a worn freighter's hat that nearly covered his eyes. Once in the room, he rotated a chaw of tobacco to one cheek and displayed a toothy grin.

'Good of you to see me, Mr Locke,' he said. 'Name's G.M. Hennesy, but most folks call me G.H. or Grady.'

'I only hire the most capable men to work for me, Grady,' Locke told the man.

'Then I'm your man, Mr Locke.' Grady chuckled. 'I've been in more scrapes than a barber's razor.'

'What brings you to Yuma?'

'The judge in San Francisco gave me a one-way ticket up here. He figured I wouldn't spend the money to buy a ticket and return.'

Grady chuckled. 'Guess he was tired of look-ing at my face.'

'You had some trouble, huh?'

'I like to think of it as more a run of bad luck.'

'Tell me about it.'

Grady scratched his head thoughtfully. 'You want I should start when I got caught stealing a neighbor's chicken? I was maybe eleven at the time. Then I swapped horses with some fellow and learned he had given me a stolen horse. I believe I was sixteen about then. And there has been the occa-sional dispute over a gal at saloon.' He showed a salacious grin. 'I favor the ladies some and it often comes back to boot me in the rump, if you know what I mean?

'Shucks, this one time the gal turned out to be married...' he threw up his hands. 'I didn't know it at the time. She didn't have no brand on her hip.' He shrugged his shoulders. 'Trouble is her husband was the town mayor.' Pausing, he gave a cynical shake of his head. 'Men who marry a woman so much younger than themselves shouldn't allow the gal out alone. I mean, how's a fellow to tell?'

'And what happened in San Francisco?' Locke wanted to know.

'It was a slight misunderstanding over a

Chinese girl.'

'A Chinese girl?'

Grady took on a meek expression and explained how he discovered the girl frightened and hiding from someone. He didn't learn till later that she belonged to one of the tongs! He grunted at that point in his story.

'Make that two tongs ... and both laid claim to the poor girl! I reckon you know Chinese girls are near as scarce as a snake with shoulders. Anyhow, each side claimed her and I kind of ended up in the middle. Whilst merely defending myself, several of them high-binders ended up in the local hospital. The judge figured if he didn't get me out of town or put me in jail, I'd be dead in a week.' Another snort. 'So here I am.'

'I lost a man on the steamboat, Lard Ackers.' Lock got down to business. 'Maybe you got to know him?'

'Sizeable sort,' Grady said, with an affirmative nod of his head. 'We didn't share whiskey or break bread together, but I seen him around.'

'How about the salesman who killed him?'

Grady showed a silly grin. 'We didn't spend a lot of time together, but I did have a look at the drawings he had of some women's frilly unmentionables in his catalog. 'Course I was pretending to be looking for something for myself. The price of a pair long-handles seemed right fair, but who needs them in this here part of the country?'

'That's a good point.'

'Anyhow, a guy over at the saloon told me how Lard drove wagon for you,' Grady said. 'Probably ain't a decent thing to do, asking for a dead man's job, but a feller has got to eat.'

'You have experience as a teamster?'

Grady replied, 'I drove stagecoach for a year or so, hauled ore for a silver-mine operation up near Leadville, Colorado, plus I spent some time hauling freight for the railroad. I can handle a wagon or team of most any size.'

Locke studied the man for a moment. Lean, weathered, in his mid-thirties; he wore his gun as if he knew how to use it and his clothes matched those of a teamster. Even if he didn't need him for anything special, the man could deliver to the nearby farmers and ranchers. It would free up one of his more trusted men.

'Do you have eating money?' he asked.

'I've enough coins to tide me over for a spell.'

Locke nodded his approval. 'I pay the first

of every month, if you need a place to stay, you can bunk with my hired help. Talk to the man in charge – Mort Lindsay.'

'Met him on the boat,' Grady said. 'He seems an OK sort.'

'Long as you do your job we'll get along just fine,' Locke told him.

'I'm an able hand, Mr Locke, that's a fact.'

'Tell Mort I sent you and he'll find you a place to stow your gear. Welcome to my small group of employees, Grady.'

'Thank you, Mr Locke,' Grady said, showing a natural grin, 'I'll make a special effort to see you don't regret hiring me.'

As soon as Grady had left the room Locke returned to his vigil. The marshal and Valenteen had parted company. The lawman headed for his office, while Valenteen entered the saddle shop. He still had a bad feeling about that man.

About to return to his desk, he spied his own reflection from the window glass. Luck had been riding his shoulder when he arrived in Yuma. Ending up with a store, suddenly respectable and all, it was a real change from his wandering days. He wasn't about to let someone upset his plans, especially some nosy salesman.

He'd lost a trusted employee in Lard

Ackers – dumb as a box of rocks, but loyal as a hound dog. A wagon mishap had cost him a man only a few weeks back, so he was running short-handed. He had only Bung, Mort and Flint to rely on for his special jobs. Henry, his night watchman, could be trusted, but he needed another man or two. He would keep an eye on Grady and see how he worked out. It was a delicate time for him and his plans for the future. The load of rifles was his chance to really make some money, but the risk was great.

Thinking of the money he would make, Locke rubbed his hands together. He had put a fair amount of cash away and this sale would add to it nicely. Time was not on his side, as the years had been hard on him, but he knew what he wanted. Once he had enough money, he would bid adieu to this hot part of the country and be gone like a puff of smoke. He would set down roots in a new place, find himself a willing bride and live out his years in style and luxury. That's all he wanted.

He firmed his resolve. A few more major sales would make his dreams all come to pass. Now that the wandering bands of Comanche and Apache were wise to stealing money and gold, the price for his rifles would add to his stash. Everything he'd worked for was at stake. All he needed was a few more deliveries to reach his goal.

'You better be as straight as an Apache arrow, Valenteen,' he said, gazing down at the man in front of the saddle shop. 'No one is going to ruin my plans.'

CHAPTER FOUR

Clay recognized the type of man at once – hat tilted off to the side, a natural swagger to his gait, fairly tall, with a handsome face and neatly trimmed moustache. The pearl-handled gun on his hip glistened in the evening sunset. His boots were polished, tailor-made, with colored rhinestones up the sides. He was a dandy with the ladies, no doubt about it.

'Say, bucko?' the fancy gent asked, stopping in front of Clay. 'You wouldn't happen to know where I could find the little gal who arrived by riverboat with you?'

'You mean Miss Haversack?'

'She's the one.' A cocky smirk entered his expression. 'I need to make amends for a little misunderstanding betwixt the two of us.'

'Misunderstanding,' Clay repeated the word. 'You mean about how you sweet talked a virtuous young girl into running away from home with your lying promise of marriage?'

The grin faded at once. 'Easy, bucko. I only tell the ladies what they want to hear. It isn't my fault if they mistake a few sweet words for a lifelong commitment.'

'You're the kind of man who slinks through life lower than a snail's belly, Cooner,' Clay told him bluntly. 'I wouldn't tell you where to find the nearest water if your trousers were on fire.'

Flint's expression darkened. 'How'd you know my name?'

'Simple,' Clay replied, fixing him with a hard stare, 'I asked around as to who was the most sleazy, scum-wallowing maggot in town and everyone answered the same – Flint Cooner.'

Flint didn't reply, but he did telegraph his move. When he swung his fist at Clay's head, Clay was prepared. He threw up his left arm and blocked the punch, then quickly drove his right fist squarely into Flint's face. His knuckles exploded at the base of the man's nose and he felt the bone crack.

The blow rocked Flint's head back and knocked off his hat. He was blinded by the rush of tears to his eyes and blood immediately began to run from his nose. He lifted his guard to protect his face, only to have the wind driven from his lungs by two solid blows to his stomach. He back-pedaled trying to escape, but Clay was a raging storm. He unleashed a fury of blows, raining down on him like a cloud burst, hammering him in the ribs, stomach and about the head. He didn't let up until the man sank down to his knees.

Dazed and unable to fight back, Flint swayed there, arms loose at his sides, his exposed, bloody face open for a final shot.

Instead of taking advantage of his helpless situation, Clay grabbed a handful of the man's hair, yanked his head back and issued a stern warning.

'If I hear that you've said so much as "good day" to Miss Haversack, I'll finish this, Flint. You hear me?'

Flint's eyes were glassy and his mouth hung open inanely, but he managed a minute nod. Clay released his hold and Flint toppled over onto his back, where he lay on the ground sucking in gulps of air, trying to recover his senses.

Clay grunted with disgust and strode over to a nearby watering trough, where he began to wash traces of blood from his knuckles. He paused to scrutinize his shirt front, observing several crimson spots.

'There goes a perfectly good clean shirt,' he muttered.

'I been waitin' to see thet ever since Crooner done drawed his first breath in Yuma,' an old gent spoke up. 'One gal he sugar-talked ended up in the family way and he sent her packin'!'

'Yeah,' added a second, patting Clay on the back, 'it's high time someone cleaned his pipe. Good job, sonny.'

Once finished at the trough and being congratulated by onlookers, Clay turned and walked toward the hotel. He had used a little water to remove most of the red stains from his shirt, but now it would need time to dry.

Clay returned to his room and removed and laid out the shirt to dry. He donned his only change of shirt and was doing up the buttons when a tap came at the door. He automatically pulled the gun from his holster. Flint might have some friends who had come to even the score.

However, when he cracked the door for a peek, he spied Billy Jo. She was alone and appeared awkward and uncertain. Clay opened the door wide and regarded her with a curious stare.

'Little britches?' he said curiously.

The girl squirmed under his gaze. 'I ... do you know who that was? The man you fought with out in the street?'

Clay was nonchalant. 'Just some dandy who thought he could push people around,' he replied.

A narrow suspicion entered Billy Jo's eyes. 'His name is Flint Cooner.'

Clay shrugged off the information. 'Are you working for the newspaper now?' he asked. 'Is that what this visit is about, you want a story?'

A crimson hue oozed upward to color her cheeks. 'I think you knew who he was,' she stated firmly. 'You beat him up because of how he made a fool out of me.'

'Why should I care one way or another about your relationship with him?'

Tight frown lines formed at the corners of her mouth. 'I think you do care!' she declared. 'And it don't set right.' In a huff, she blurted, 'Tell me why you fought with him!'

Clay stepped back into the room. 'Want to come in?'

'I'm not going to enter a man's hotel

room.' Then, as an afterthought, considering she had spent the night in that very room, 'Not while you're here anyway.'

Clay tucked in his shirt and picked up his jacket. 'I was on my way to get something to eat,' he offered. 'How about you join me?'

'No thanks.'

'I still owe you a meal, remember?'

Billy Jo lowered her gaze once more. 'You don't owe me anything.'

'Come on,' he coaxed. 'I've got an idea about a job for you.'

The girl did not answer, but Clay slipped on his jacket and exited the room. Once in the hallway, he took her by the arm and started to walk.

'I don't want to be further in debt to you,' she vowed. 'I can make my own way.'

'Fair enough,' he replied. 'We can discuss your future over a meal.'

Clay led the way to Etta's Eating Emporium where he chose a table off in a corner. It was a little early for most diners, so the place wasn't overly busy.

Etta was a hefty woman, nearly as wide as she was tall, but she had a pleasant face and ready smile.

'Good day, folks,' she greeted them. 'My own recipe – son-of-a-gun stew – is the special today, served up with hard rolls and whatever you want to drink. Four-bits each.'

Clay looked at Billy Jo and waited for her to order. 'That will be fine,' she said. 'And lemonade, if you have some.'

'We even have ice,' Etta returned, 'but it's two cents extra.'

'Bring us two glasses of lemonade with ice,' Clay told her. 'And I'll also have a plate of your stew.'

Etta bobbed her head and waddled toward the kitchen to get the order. As soon as she was out of hearing distance, Billy Jo cleared her throat.

'I'll pay you back for this.'

'Not necessary,' he replied. 'I promised you payment for helping me out with the guard last night. You don't owe me anything.'

'Except the money for the trip up here by steamship,' she reminded him.

'How would you like to pay that off?'

The girl frowned. 'What are you up to, Mr Valenteen? What do you want from me?'

'Not a thing,' he said placidly. 'I've got a job for you.'

A wariness entered the girls' expression. 'Yeah? Doing what?'

'Catalog sales,' he answered. 'How would you like to go around to the different businesses and homes and take orders? You get a commission for every sale and, depending upon how many sales you make, you could earn enough money to maybe pay off some of your debt too.'

Billy Jo displayed a puzzled expression. 'Why would you need someone to do sales for you? Are you really a salesman or are you up to something else?'

'Something else?' Clay feigned innocence.

'Why did you need to look in that storage warehouse?' she asked. 'And what were you looking for in the cargo hold of the ship?'

'I have out-of-town customers I need to speak to,' he said, dismissing her suspicions. 'My idea is, if you were to help with the local stuff, I could finish the job that much sooner.'

'You're more than a salesman for some back East store,' she stated confidently, not dissuaded by his sidestep. 'And I sure don't aim to get involved in something that might get me thrown in jail or killed.'

Etta returned with their meal and lemonade. It allowed for the girl to consider his proposal. As soon as they were alone, he took a sip from his glass and heaved a sigh.

'Ah-h-h,' he said, 'a cold drink sure tastes good in all of this heat.'

Billy Jo also took a sip of her lemonade, then a second. 'Um-m,' she agreed, 'I've never had ice in a drink before.' Then, showing a hint of a smile, 'At least, not that I remember.'

'You didn't say where you came from,' Clay pointed out.

'No,' was her soft reply.

'You must be running from something pretty bad.'

The girl picked up her fork and stabbed a cube of potato from the stew. 'We were talking about you,' she reminded him. 'You were going to tell me what you are up to.'

Clay smiled at her. 'It seems we are both keeping secrets from one another. How about we stick to business?'

The girl chewed ravenously and speared another chunk from the stew. Billy Jo was obviously famished. Even so, she continued to converse. 'I don't know nothing about selling from a catalog.'

'Can you read and do your numbers?'

'I went to school,' she replied. Then added between mouthfuls, 'Long enough to learn my letters and do my sums.'

'The job isn't difficult to learn. Most of the time you only have to be cordial and allow people to decide if there is something they want to buy. The merchandise sells itself. Your job is to do the paperwork and collect the money.'

Billy Jo appeared to do some thinking, while chewing on a tough bite of stew meat. After a long pause, she looked him straight in the eye.

'All right, Mr Valenteen,' she said. 'I'm not making any promises, but I'll try this catalog sales thing for a couple days and see how it goes. Fair enough?'

'Fair enough.'

Locke studied Flint's bruised and swollen face. 'You look like you were kicked by a mule.'

'I can believe that drummer took Lard in a fight, Locke. He has some skill with his fists. I'd had a couple drinks, but nothing to slow me down. I took one swing and he was all over me like a dust devil from hell.'

'I assume you didn't get to question the girl.' It was a statement.

'Valenteen warned me not to try and contact her again.' Flint touched the side of his puffy nose and grimaced. 'I'd as soon not get on his bad side a second time.'

'What we need is some leverage, something to bring the girl to us.' Locke began to pace.

'Your cousin is going to be here to arrange shipment of goods in the next day or two. You know how Banty is, Flint. He will expect delivery within a couple days. We're running out of time and I don't like loose ends.'

'I can reason with Banty if we need an extra day or two.'

'It's hard to believe you two are related,' Locke said. 'Banty hasn't got a drop of blood in his veins. The man is made out of ice.'

'We didn't get along much as kids,' Flint admitted. 'He was the fighter and I was the lover.' He showed a crooked grin. 'Some things don't change.'

'All right, so let's deal with the salesman and eliminate that worry.'

'We ain't seen a shred of proof that this guy is anything more than an order-taker for the Grange Supply House,' Flint pointed out. 'Could be we're worrying for no reason.'

'I spoke to Judge Stickley about him. He didn't charge Valenteen with Lard's murder 'cause the girl spoke up and said it was a fair fight.'

'Mort told me about it,' Flint said. 'He found Lard's knife and tossed it overboard. You would think the judge would have charged him with some crime, what with there being no weapon to back up his story.'

'The girl vouched for him; the case is closed.'

'If we had gotten a thirty-day jail sentence – even a couple weeks.'

'Let it go, Flint. That much is over and done with.'

'If you say so.'

'Judge Stickley didn't buy the fellow as being a mere salesman either.' Locke made a face. 'Something tells me this guy is bad news for us and we can't afford any mistakes.'

'So we do it right,' Flint suggested. 'Let Bung push him into a gunfight and we'll be rid of him once and for sure!'

'If he is some kind of lawman, killing him would bring a dozen badges up here. We don't want to stir up more trouble.'

Flint suddenly smiled. 'Wouldn't be no questions asked, if the drummer was the one to start the fight.'

'Why would he be the one to start a fight?'

Flint hooked a thumb at his battered face. 'Same reason he did this to me.'

'You have a plan?'

'Trust me, Locke.' Flint began to chuckle. 'Yes, sir, I know just what we need to bring our buzzing bee to the hive.'

Locke crossed his arms. 'All right, give me the details.'

To maintain his cover, Clay spoke to Baxter and had him map the outlying farms and ranches. He would ride out early each morning and visit a couple, then slip back to a point where he could keep watch over the comings and goings at the warehouse. It was obvious Locke was involved. The crates were shipped to his store and placed in his warehouse. But he needed to know who the contact person was, the one who dealt directly with the Indians. It wasn't enough to procure the guns, he had to shut down the pipeline between the smugglers and the weapon suppliers.

On his ride out of town, he made a point of passing next to the warehouse. It allowed him to make a subtle inspection of the tracks around the entrance. There had been no rain in recent weeks, but the powdery dust was matted only by boot and hoof prints. There was no sign of recent wagon tracks.

Clay left town and headed for the first ranch on his map. The solitude of the ride allowed him time to consider options and retrace the ground he had covered.

The stolen army rifles'd come a long way. He had followed their trail since they were reported missing. Earmarked for delivery to two different forts, the shipment had come from back East and disappeared *en route* between Saint Louis and Denver. Sixty rifles, Model '73 Winchesters, along with several thousand rounds of ammunition, enough firepower to prolong the Indian campaigns for months. Given the newer weapons, the Apache would be equipped to confound and possibly defeat a much larger force of soldiers, many of whom still carried the old-fashioned bolt-action or single-shot carbines.

On one hand, Clay felt compassion for the renegade Apache and Comanche band – especially the small bunch suspected of attacking settlers around Yuma. They had lived under Cochise, one of the great leaders of the Apache. He had signed a treaty which gave his people title to the land which they had occupied for many years. The reservation was their home, with only set boundaries to limit the hunting and travel of his people. When Cochise died, some land-hungry mongrels pressured the government to have the reservation moved to San Carlos, a strip of barren desert where even the scorpion could not thrive. This latest band to run off from the reservation had raided and pillaged its way across Arizona, traveling over 200 miles to wind up buying guns in

Yuma. Moving those Apache to San Carlos was shameful, yet there was nothing the ordinary man could do. For the various tribes of Indians, their plight was no different than any other side which lost a war, they had to make the best of what they were given. It was either that or fight and die.

Some might have acknowledged the fairness of providing the over-matched and out-numbered Indians with new rifles. It was hard not to be supportive of any group that was fighting an impossible battle against impossible odds. However, the outcome of the Indian rebellion was not in question, only the time frame and number of lives which would be lost. In truth, the only thing accomplished by providing the renegade force with new weapons was that the fight would last longer, and more settlers, soldiers and Indians would die in the process.

What stuck in Clay's craw were the few greedy traitors. They bore no concern for fairness or charity. They were making a great amount of money at the cost of numerous lives on both sides. If ever the label of 'blood money' fitted a group of low-life vermin, it was well suited to the men who sold guns to the Indians.

Clay managed a few sales at the two

ranches he visited, but there were only a couple of women at either place. He had found that women were the best customers, especially in remote regions. They were usually restricted to buying only what was offered at the nearby trading post or general store. With so few female customers, most local businesses didn't carry a lot of frills or goods for women. The catalog allowed them the rare opportunity to buy a variety of items and also offered an assortment of sizes and colors.

Always vigilant, Clay was certain he had been followed as far as the first ranch. He saw no one on his back trail after that. He assumed someone was keeping an eye on him long enough to see that he was actually doing sales. Once convinced of his mission, they either returned to town to report or found themselves a shady spot and awaited his return.

The thought of shade was foremost in Clay's mind as the mid-morning sun began to beat down unmercifully. Trapped between the oppressive rays from the sun and the reflective heat from the earth's crust, Clay felt an empathy with a nearly baked rump roast.

With his hat tipped to shade his face, he would appear casual to an observer, but his eyes never ceased movement. The waves of heat distorted objects in the distance, so any ambush would likely come at close range. Not that he expected trouble, unless it was from a couple of renegade Indians or starving bandits, but there was an outside chance Locke, or whoever had control of the guns, might decide he was a risk. He tried not to give anyone reason to suspect his movements, though killing Lard Ackers had definitely put him under scrutiny. Add to that misfortune he had dished out a healthy dose of punishment to Flint Cooner. Fighting with two of Locke's men was not exactly the best method for remaining inconspicuous.

Returning to town, Clay retraced his path, riding close enough to the warehouse to survey the ground. There were no new wagon tracks. The guns were still there.

Billy Jo appeared, exiting from the barber and bath, located next to the general store. She had a fistful of papers in her hand and a very businesslike look on her face. Her earnest expression caused Clay to smile. She was a determined young woman. A person who stowed away in the cargo hold of a ship, suffered temperatures well over a hundred, locked in total darkness, eating and drinking who knows what to survive – that person had some perseverance.

Billy Jo turned in the direction of another store, but stopped when she spied Clay. For the first time since he had met the girl, a natural smile curled her lips and she lifted a hand and waved.

Clay pulled up his rented horse at the nearest hitching post and climbed down. The girl moved quickly to arrive at his side.

'Look here!' she said proudly. 'Sixty-four dollars' worth of orders!'

Clay blinked in surprise. 'Holy Hannah, gal!' he exclaimed. 'That's a fair day's work and it's not much past noon.'

'And I earn five per cent, is that right?'

'You bet. You're already, uh' – he multiplied in his head – 'three dollars and twenty cents to the good. That's about a full week's wages for a housekeeper or waitress.'

'And the laundry woman said she might order more. She has to talk to her husband first. I'm supposed to go back to see her tomorrow.'

Clay smiled broadly. 'Little britches, I'm truly amazed. You've made as many sales today as I have since I hit town.'

The girl's eyes positively sparkled with delight. She stood erect, displaying a new pride in herself.

'I only did what you told me,' she said, allowing him a portion of the credit. 'I let each customer look at the pages without rushing them, then told them how they could rely on the Grange Supply House to ship them exactly what they ordered. The barber didn't need no coaxing, cause he was familiar with the company and knew what he wanted.'

Clay didn't mention that he had visited the barber and showed him the catalog the previous day. He let Billy Jo take the credit, feeling good inside for giving her the chance to gain some confidence.

'We need to celebrate,' Clay said. 'I'm buying you lunch.'

'If you're taking me to eat at Etta's, I'm not going to order the son-of-a-gun stew again.'

He chuckled, tying off his horse. 'No, you can order anything you want.'

As they started toward Etta's Eating Emporium, Billy Jo fell in alongside Clay. She began to talk excitedly about visiting the other business owners and some of the nearby houses. It was the first time she had let her guard down and actually conversed as if they were friends.

They ordered a meal and continued to talk back and forth. Clay found himself delighting in her enthusiasm and soon they were joking and laughing together. The girl was as different from the somber, taciturn stowaway as night from day.

That's when Bung entered the room.

Clay spotted him at once. It didn't take a heavenly inspiration to know the gunman had come looking for him. Bung paused to ease both of his guns up from his holsters and let them drop back gently to rest. Clay carefully slipped his hand down to remove the thong from his gun. Keeping his hand under the table, he laced his fingers around the butt and lifted the pistol onto his lap. He had always been good with a gun, but he was no fast draw artist. If it came to a gunfight, Clay intended to use whatever advantage he needed to win the contest.

CHAPTER FIVE

Bung approached to within ten feet of the table and stopped. 'I've been looking for you, you shifty little gallnipper,' he drawled to Billy Jo.

The girl displayed surprise and an instant

displeasure. 'I'm not a mosquito.'

'Way I hear it, you sucked the blood right out of your pa and brothers,' he continued to taunt the girl.

'Why are you looking for the lady?' Clay interjected, displaying a neutral smile. 'You fixing to buy something from the Grange Supply House?'

A dark light danced within the man's eyes. 'There's a bounty on the little 'skeeto here,' Bung sneered the words, 'and it's a sizeable amount.'

Billy Jo flashed a mystified glance at Clay and regarded Bung a blank stare.

'I don't know what you are talking about.'

The gunman's lips curled upward, revealing a mouthful of crooked teeth. He spoke to Billy Jo, but he paid keen attention to Clay's every move.

'You didn't think Dutch would let you run away without even looking for you?' he asked.

The name caused Billy Jo to catch her breath. Her eyes widened in alarm and all color seemed to drain from her face. She shook her head back and forth. 'No!' she declared vehemently, 'I don't believe it!'

'Oh, yes, little missy,' Bung mocked her with a stinging tone. 'You're worth a thousand dollars to me.'

Billy Jo shrank back and continued shaking her head. 'You've made a mistake.'

'No mistake,' Bung retorted. 'You cheated a man named Dutch out of something that was properly pledged to him and he wants that property returned.' He grinned, 'That would be you, gallnipper.'

'I'm not an insect, nor am I anyone's property!' Billy Jo cried. 'Dutch is a dirty old man who wanted to buy himself a bride.' She jumped to her feet, face flushed with ire. 'And I won't be bought or sold like a prize horse!'

Bung gave an off-hand shrug. 'Don't much matter what you have to say, missy. You and me are taking a stage ride tomorrow ... all the way back home to Jonas Brown.'

Billy Jo swung about to plead her case to Clay. 'Jonas isn't my father!' she cried. 'He worked me like a slave for my keep and a place to live. He's no relation to me at all!'

'Stop your bawling, whelp,' Bung jeered, 'you're bringing tears to my eyes.'

'Please, Mr Valenteen,' she continued her plea, 'I'm eighteen years old. I want a say in my own life. Please don't let this man take me back to that horrible pig farmer. He's forty years old and as fat and ugly as his pigs. I can't stand the idea of him touching me. Please!'

Bung took a step forward and grabbed Billy Jo by the wrist. 'Let's go pack your things, missy. No need making a big fuss about something once it's been settled.'

Clay remained seated his hand resting on his lap with the Colt ready for use.

'Take your hand off of the young lady, bounty hunter,' he warned icily. 'Believe me when I say you don't want to push this.'

A rush of anticipation transformed the man's smirk into a deadly sneer. His right hand gripped the butt of his gun while he held on to Billy Jo with his left. Watching the dark light shimmer within the man's eyes, Clay realized the bounty had been a ruse. Bung's real objective had been to force him in to a gunfight.

'I'm going to kill you, drummer,' Bung slurred the words menacingly. 'You might as well tell me what your real purpose is in coming to Yuma.'

'Before you draw down on me,' Clay began, 'you should know that—'

He intended to remove the gun from his lap to dissuade Bung from going forward with a fight. However, at the flinch of his shoulder Bung yanked his own pistol free—

Billy Jo screamed and jerked away from him.

There was no time for words! Clay whipped up his Colt and pulled the trigger a mere instant before Bung could bring his gun to bear. The bullet struck the man near the top of his throat. The shock and force of the slug tearing through his neck knocked the gun from his hand.

Billy Jo backed away so quickly, she fell over her chair and landed sitting down on the floor.

Clay upended the table as he rose to his feet, pistol cocked, ready to fire again.

But a second shot wasn't necessary. Bung folded to his knees, grasping his injured throat with both hands. Unable to speak, Bung gasped and labored to draw a breath. Failing to suck any air into his lungs, he glowered at Clay through hate-filled eyes, until the strength left his body. After a few seconds, he pitched forward, face-down and lay still on the hard-pack dirt floor.

Five minutes later Marshal Baxter arrived. He listened to the statements of the witnesses and they all concurred, Bung had come looking to start trouble. As for who drew first, none of them had seen how Clay's gun was out and ready for use. The spectators all assumed Clay had drawn first, but he had been at the disadvantage of sitting down, so they figured that made it a fair fight.

Baxter thanked everyone in the room and had the body moved over to the undertaker. As the blood-soaked earth was covered over with a few handfuls of sawdust, the marshal pulled Clay off to one side to speak to him.

'You sure didn't stay out of trouble very long, Valenteen,' he said.

'I didn't want a fight, Marshal. I was trying to reason with Bung when he went for his gun.'

'What's this about a reward for the girl?'

'Some pig farmer named Dutch wants Billy Jo for his bride,' Clay replied. 'Bung claimed he had offered a bounty for her return.'

'You figure it's a lawful claim?'

'Billy Jo says her guardian isn't a blood relation, only a guy who made a slave of her for ten years and then decided to sell her to a wealthy pig farmer.'

'Guess we solved the mystery of why she stowed away on board the steamship,' Baxter said.

'Yeah, to escape being enslaved for life.'

Baxter uttered a sigh. 'Well, my first concern here ain't about her, it's about how I can explain to Judge Stickley that there's no sense in charging you with a second killing. Every witness I could find says it was self defense.'

'Somehow, I don't think the judge is going to be real happy about that,' Clay spoke the obvious.

'No, he won't,' Baxter agreed. He took a step toward the door, stopped and cocked his head over his shoulder at Clay. 'You sure you ain't ready to leave town? I'd buy something from your catalog myself to be rid of you.'

'A couple more days are all I need.'

Baxter groaned. 'Let's see, that means only killing one or two more men. I guess that isn't so bad. Leastways, you haven't killed anyone I liked ... not yet anyhow!'

The marshal's shoulders drooped as he left the building and headed down the street to inform Stickley about Bung's death.

Billy Jo had given Clay and Baxter room to talk. She returned to stand next to Clay. He could tell she was still a bit shaken.

'I'm sorry, Mr Valenteen,' she murmured softly. 'I didn't think Jonas and Dutch would put up a reward for my return.'

'So you're a runaway bride?'

The words put the fire back into her persona. 'I never said I would marry that ... that man!' she fumed. 'Those two dirty old men arranged everything. They bargained for me like I was a horse. As soon as I learned what was in store for me, I ran away. When I reached the coast, I saw a chance to get aboard the boat and escape. I wanted to get far enough away that neither of those wretched men would ever find me again.'

'How do you suppose they learned you were here?'

Billy Jo clenched her teeth in anger. 'Only one man in town knows where I lived.'

'Flint Cooner,' Clay stated the obvious.

'But it makes no sense,' she reasoned. 'If there really is a bounty, why didn't Flint try to collect it himself?'

'I would wager Flint is no better with a pistol than he is with his fists. Bung was supposed to be the bad man in a gunfight.'

At his explanation, Billy Jo regarded Clay with a probing stare. 'The reward was only an excuse to get you to fight!' she deduced. 'Flint and Bung expected you to stick up for me!'

Clay avoided her scrutiny and gave a non-chalant shrug. 'Don't go riding a wild horse down a blind canyon, little britches. A thousand dollars is a huge reward – two or three years' wages for most men. Bung likely figured I wouldn't be fool enough to take him on.'

'He could have grabbed me any time he wanted all morning,' Billy Jo continued her argument. 'Why wait until you returned from visiting the outlying ranches?'

'Maybe word of the reward didn't come until after I returned to town.'

'Or else I'm right and this isn't about me at all!'

'Of course, it's about you.'

Billy Jo held her ground and pointed a finger at Clay's chest. 'I think you're lying, Mr Valenteen! Someone wants you dead and this was a way to draw you in to a fight.'

Clay waved a dismissive hand. 'You're making a house out of sawdust. Why should anyone want me dead?'

'Why did you have me distract that night guard so you could look in that storehouse? What were you doing in the hold of the ship, attempting to pry open a crate addressed to someone else? Why does everything about you being a salesman seem completely phoney?' She uttered her triumphant conclusion, 'That gunman was here for you!'

Clay was trapped by the truth, but gave a last-ditch effort to change her mind.

'You're reaching way over your head, little britches. Why would Bung and Flint use the story about taking you home to get me to fight? They couldn't have possibly known that I would stand up for you.'

Billy Jo stared at him for a long moment and an odd change took place. Her rigid determination melted away to a subtle tenderness. The appearance reminded Clay of the way a woman's expression changed whenever they looked upon or held a newborn baby. With the staunch resolution in her make-up dissolved, she demurely lowered her head.

'They knew you'd fight for me,' she murmured.

'How could they know something like that?'

'You paid my fare so I wouldn't get taken back on the steamship,' she said softly. 'You gave me your room so I wouldn't have to sleep in a barn; you tried to keep me out of trouble at the saloon; you beat Flint like a dusty rug because of me; you've even given me a job.' She turned her head slightly from side to side. 'You have been taking such good care of me' – she lifted her eyes to study him – 'maybe I should be worrying about your intentions.'

Clay didn't reply to her list of events, but reached down to right the table, which had remained overturned. He paid for their meal, added a couple dollars for damages and led Billy Jo out of the eating emporium. He paused at the street to look both ways. If Locke had sent Bung to force a fight, it could mean the man was about to move the rifles. If he became overly concerned about who Clay was and what he knew he might order an ambush. From now on, Clay would have to be extra careful.

'What are we going to do?' Billy Jo asked, when Clay failed to respond to her last comment. 'Someone wants you dead. And if there really is such a large reward for my return, a great number of men might come looking for me.'

'As for my situation, I'll be careful,' he answered eventually. 'But for you, little britches, it's time you decided to trust me.'

'Trust you?'

'There is a law against putting a price on someone's head to have them kidnapped. If you tell me the whole truth about your home, your guardian and this guy Dutch, then maybe we can get the bounty removed.'

Billy Jo appeared uncertain. 'I have lived by my wits since I was a little girl, Mr Valenteen,' she explained quietly. 'I have not trusted anyone but myself. I couldn't take the chance. No one cared what happened to me.'

'I cared enough to kill a man on your

behalf,' he reminded her. 'Even if Bung's intention was to push me into a fight, I still prevented him from taking you. That ought to mean something.'

'It does,' she admitted. 'And you have proven yourself to be a complete gentleman at every turn' – with a slight simper breaking her somber mood – 'except for when you forced me to take a bath in the jail cell.'

'Yes, well, unlike you, I didn't know you weren't a man when I took my bath!'

'I didn't peek,' she avowed. 'It wouldn't have been right.'

'And I returned the favor,' he reciprocated. Then, allowing a mischievous grin, 'But I might have had second thoughts, had I known there was such a pretty young lady under those dirty old rags.'

Rather than outrage or offense, Billy Jo giggled. 'It's funny to hear you refer to me as a young lady.'

A warm tremor nudged Clay's heart at seeing and hearing the girl laugh. Of course it could have been the hundred-degree heat, but he could not deny there was something very special about Billy Jo.

'What do you say?' he returned to business. 'We can talk to the judge together.'

'You would do that for me?'

'Better than getting in another fight over you,' Clay told her. 'Don't you agree?'

Billy Jo blushed. 'Yes, of course.'

He grew serious and looked directly into her eyes.

'I swear to you, little britches, you can trust me.'

Billy Jo took a deep breath and expelled it slowly.

'All right, Mr Valenteen,' she said quietly, 'let's go talk to the judge.'

Warren Locke stormed about the room, waving his hands in the air and cursing with every step.

'How could this have happened?' he bellowed at Flint. 'You said Valenteen was a no account with a gun!'

'He sure don't wear a gun like a man who knows much about using it,' Flint whined. 'And he risked damaging his hands when he and I mixed it up. A smart gunman don't jeopardize busting a knuckle on his gun hand by fighting with his fists.'

'Tell that to Bung!' Locke snarled. 'Your idea has cost me a second man, one I could ill-afford to lose!'

'Maybe we ought to back-shoot the man from ambush and be done with it.'

'Good thinking,' Locke snorted his disdain. 'If Valenteen is working for the army, killing him would bring every lawman from a thousand miles down on us!'

'So what are we going to do?' Flint asked.

Locke stopped at the window. 'There's the salesman now.' He uttered a grunt. 'He and that little hellion are going to visit the judge.'

'You think he knows?' Flint worried. 'If the judge gives him a warrant or something, he can arrest us on the spot.'

'He wouldn't take the girl with him for that,' Locke said. 'I'm betting this is about the bounty on the girl.'

'Yeah,' Flint agreed, immediately relieved, 'that makes sense. They sure don't want anyone else coming to collect.'

'Meanwhile, we're short a driver,' Locke got back to business. 'With Lard and Bung both dead, I don't have anyone I can trust to deliver the load to your cousin.'

'Mort can do the deal same as always. Banty knows him.'

'Yes, but he always had Lard and Bung at his side,' Locke reminded Flint. 'Mort can't handle the transfer by himself. The wagon needs an armed escort of at least two riders.'

'How about that new guy you hired?' he asked.

Locke grunted. 'I don't know anything about Grady. I hired him to do the local deliveries.'

'You've got Henry, the night guard at the storehouse.'

'I've got a couple of employees running my store too, Flint. You think I ought to send Mrs. Davis with Mort? Or maybe you'd like to hire the town runner, Jules?'

'Don't get sore, boss,' Flint whined a second time. 'I'm only saying I could cover for Henry, the night before the delivery, so he could get some sleep. Then he could join Mort.'

'We're getting pretty damn thin on help,' Locke growled the words. 'I need to find some new men to replace the hired hands we've lost! How am I going to make this delivery?'

'It will work out for this one trip,' Flint replied carefully. 'I'll watch Valenteen while Mort and Henry make the run.'

'That Valenteen is a walking curse,' Locke sneered. 'If I were a historian, I would name a plague after him.'

'I'm telling you, boss, if Mort and Henry do the loading and unloading of the crates, Grady won't even know what's in the wagon.'

Locke wrinkled his brow at the idea so Flint

hurried forward with his idea. 'Mort can have Grady water the team or something while he and Henry do the deal with Banty.'

Locke still didn't like the plan, but what were his options? He couldn't very well drive the wagon himself and he needed no less than two outriders to make sure the wagon arrived at its destination safely.

'When are you setting up the exchange?'

'Banty is supposed to contact me tonight, sometime after it gets dark.'

'I don't like having those guns sitting in my warehouse, not with the chance there might be a government man snooping around.'

'Valenteen could be just what he claims to be, boss.'

'But what if he's not!' Locke snapped back. 'When a wandering salesman kills two of my men I tend to be mistrustful of his motives.'

'Mort and me will keep an eye on him until the delivery.'

Locke bobbed his head affirmatively. 'All right, but be sure to watch him from a distance. I can't afford the loss of another man.'

Flint said they would be careful and left the room. Locke watched him leave, then went over to his liquor cabinet and poured himself a drink. He didn't stop at his usual two-fingers but filled the glass nearly to the brim. This situation was growing more dangerous by the minute. He gulped down a large swallow. The liquor burned his throat and brought tears to his eyes.

Of all the foul, rotten luck! He swore vehemently.

This was the first time in his life that he had ever had anything he could call his own. Two or three more shipments of guns and he would have all the money he needed. He was so close. He took another jolt of the whiskey and vented his ire a second time.

'Damn you, Valenteen! Lawman or just plain lousy troublemaker, you're ruining everything I've worked for!'

CHAPTER SIX

Judge Stickley was at his desk when Clay and Billy Jo entered. He looked up from his work and frowned.

'The marshal was just here to tell me you had killed another of our citizens, Mr Valenteen. Are you trying to depopulate Yuma all by yourself?'

Clay explained how the fight had come

about and the judge turned his attention to Billy Jo.

'About this bounty,' he said, 'why don't you tell me your story, young lady.'

'We were moving to California so my pa could get rich,' she began. 'At least, that's what I remember as a child. Shortly before we reached the coast we all came down with fever. The wagon-train didn't stop for stragglers, so we camped at a farming settlement named Calico Flats. My ma and pa both died so a man named Jonas Brown took me in. I was about eight years old at the time.'

Stickley gave a sympathetic nod of his head. 'Go on.'

'For ten long years, I was a personal slave to him, his crazy wife and their two ornery sons. I didn't even have a room of my own, just a corner of the back porch. In the summer it was too hot to sleep nights. During the winter, I had to sleep in my clothes to keep from freezing. This dress here, the one Marshal Baxter gave me to wear, is as nice as anything I've ever owned.'

'Sounds like a tough life,' the judge sympathized.

'The old lady was not right in the head,' Billy Jo went on. 'She would often commence to fret or cry and sometimes got violent. She

114

must have hit me a hundred times and even took after me with a knife when I spilled some milk once. Whatever was wrong with her, it finally took her life a couple of years back.'

She grimaced at the ugly memory, but continued with the narration. 'Jonas and his sons were not much better. I had to do all of the house duties, the cooking and cleaning, the laundry. When I got a little older, he hired me out to other folks to do the same for them. As for the boys, they liked to tease and torment me, trying to make me holler. I lived with those crazy critters for ten long years, up before daylight and working till dark. I was not a member of the family: I was their personal slave.'

She paused to recoup her courage, then continued.

'The two boys were three and four years older than me. When I began to ... uh ... blossom,' she colored noticeably, but kept going, 'their teasing turned more personal. I had to wash when they were all working, cause they would try and get a peek. They started grabbing or trying to touch me, so I had to fight them off. If I clawed one of his boys or hit them with something, Jonas would punish me. A time or two, when I tried to run away, he and his boys caught me and took me back for a beating. I lost count of the number of times I felt the sting of his belt.'

'And who is this Dutch character?' the judge wanted to know.

'He was the closest neighbor we had. When the wind blew from the south, we could smell his herd of pigs.' She wrinkled her nose at the memory. 'And the wind blew a lot from that direction.'

'He's the one who put up the money for your return?'

'Dutch had three or four hired hands, but there weren't a lot of girls around for marrying. Jonas and his boys barely scratched a living on the farm, but Dutch made big money raising and selling his pigs.'

'So Jonas and he got together,' the judge deduced.

'And they settled on a price for me,' she finished.

The judge was thoughtful for a moment. 'Do you have any relatives, an aunt or uncle somewhere?'

'I was only eight when my folks died,' she reminded him. 'As far as I know, I don't have anyone in the world.'

'That being the case, this Jonas might be able to lay claim as your legal guardian.' Billy

Jo started to protest, but the judge continued, 'However, I don't care for the idea of anyone being sold off like a prize heifer.'

'An arranged marriage is one thing,' Clay interjected, 'but this is different.'

'Only one option open to us,' Judge Stickley stated to Billy Jo, 'you are not of legal age so you must have a guardian.' He regarded Clay with a curious look. 'Do you know someone willing to take over the guardianship of this young woman?'

Clay felt his mouth drop open. 'I ... I...'

Stickley grinned. 'Very good! I hereby grant you custody of this young woman. You are her legally appointed custodian until she is twenty-one years old or gets married.'

'Judge, I–' Clay began.

Stickley prohibited any protest. 'Perhaps being responsible for this lady will help rein in your propensity for killing people, Mr Valenteen.' Then, more businesslike, 'Considering your new position as Miss Haversack's guardian, I will contact the marshal's office at Calico Flats. I'll instruct him to cancel the bounty offered for the young lady and break the news to both Jonas and Dutch.' He raised his bushy eyebrows. 'Questions?'

Utterly confounded, Clay could only shake his head.

Stickley snorted and waved his hand, as if shooing them away. 'I'll send the telegram off right away. Good day to you both.'

'Thank you, Judge,' Billy Jo gushed. 'Oh, thank you so much!'

'Yeah,' Clay managed begrudgingly, 'thanks a heap.'

Once outside, Clay and Billy Jo walked down the street together. Clay sought a quiet place to talk and chose a secluded spot, a short distance from the livery. The horses in the corral were seeking shelter from the hot sun, standing together in the limited amount of shade from the barn. To escape the relentless heat, Clay and Billy Jo moved over next to a tool shed. A shaded bench was located there, as this was a popular spot for horseshoe players. Two sets of pegs had been driven in to the ground some forty feet apart and the ground was dusty and churned from use. The bench was obviously there for spectators or players who paused to rest during or between games. They sat down and Clay tried to sort out his thoughts.

'It's hard to believe,' Billy Jo gushed happily, 'I'm actually free of Jonas and his sons.'

Clay rubbed the back of his neck, trying to get his brain to function. He had offered to help and ended up as the girl's guardian. He had to admit he had entertained some notions about Billy Jo, but being a father figure was not one of them.

'What's the matter?' the girl asked. 'You haven't said a word since we left the judge.'

Clay was searching for a response when he spied a man wandering out near the corral. He appeared to be tinkering with a harness, but Clay knew why he was there.

Grady!

'Sit right here for a minute, little britches,' Clay told the girl. 'I'm so dry I can hardly swallow.'

She gave him a questioning look, but didn't say anything.

Clay rose up, glanced around to be sure he wasn't being watched, then walked over to the nearby water pump. The corner of the corral extended right up next to the pump so it could be used to fill the watering trough for the horses.

Clay had to work the handle several times before the water came. The trough was nearly empty, so the pumping of water caused several horses to drift over for a drink of fresh water. Clay wet his hand and took a sip, then continued to pump enough water for the thirsty horses.

'Feel's hotter than the devil's oven today,

sonny,' Grady said, loud enough for anyone nearby to hear. 'Even them desert-born mustang nags are dying of thirst.'

'That's the truth, friend,' Clay replied.

Grady took a step in his direction and lowered his head. From the distance, it would appear he was intently working on the strap.

'Something's up, Val,' he whispered, barely moving his lips. 'Flint told me to stick close to town so I can drive a wagon out on a delivery. He was right vague about when this little trip might take place.'

Clay also spoke from the side of his mouth. 'Think it's the shipment?'

'Got to be,' he answered. 'You done kilt their two main drivers, so they are forced to use me.'

'I don't suppose the captain will see the logic of my actions.'

'No such luck,' Grady replied. 'According to him, everyone gets to tell their side of the story in court ... before we can hang them.'

Clay stopped working the pump handle and spoke up. 'That ought to hold these thirsty critters until the hostler comes around.'

Grady also raised his head and elevated his voice, 'Won't last but an hour or so in this heat.' As Clay started to walk away,

Grady whispered, 'They might be watching me, so keep a sharp eye. If I can, I'll let you know when I'm pulling out ahead of time.'

'Don't take any chances,' Clay mumbled softly. 'I'll be ready to handle my end.'

Grady held up the strap and pulled at either end. Nodding with satisfaction, he pivoted around and walked toward the barn.

Clay returned to where Billy Jo had remained sitting. She had a suspicious look on her face.

'Who's that, your father?'

'You remember him from the boat ride, don't you?'

She remained cynical. 'Never knew you two were friends.'

'He looked at my catalog on the journey up here,' Clay replied. 'He was asking how sales were.'

'And I'm to believe that, huh?' she quipped. 'Did that little speech you gave me about trust only go one way?'

Clay frowned. 'You are starting to give me a headache, little britches.'

'Telling lies can likely cause a person to suffer headaches,' was her repartee.

He couldn't pretend with Billy Jo. She had seen and witnessed too much. He decided to take her into his confidence.

'A consignment of rifles was stolen while being shipped by train,' he explained. 'They weren't the first to disappear *en route* to one of the outlying forts. You've heard of the Pinkertons, the eye that never sleeps?'

'You mean the detective agency?'

He gave a nod of his head. 'They do a lot of work for the railroad. One of their agents discovered who was behind the theft at that end. The information was turned over to us and I've been following the guns since they were taken off the train.'

'So you are a lawman.'

'I'm a federal agent, assigned to find the men who are selling guns to the Indians and stop the shipment from ending up in their hands.'

'And the guns are in the storehouse,' Billy Jo deduced.

'That's right. If the Apache get those weapons, it could lengthen the Indian war by many months and cost a great number of lives, both red and white. We have to catch the middleman, the one who is dealing directly with the Indians.'

'Then Lard and Bung were both mixed up in this.' It was a statement.

'They both worked for Warren Locke and the guns are in his warehouse. We have to assume he is the man behind dealing guns to the Indians.'

Billy Jo became pensive. Her brows drew together and a wrinkle creased her brow. 'You shouldn't be trying to help me,' she said quietly. 'You are already risking your life.'

The corners of Clay's lips turned upward. 'I don't have a choice any more.'

The frown remained in place. 'I won't hold you to being my guardian. I've been enough trouble to you already.'

'Is that what you think?'

'Yes!' she affirmed. 'I didn't speak up for you on the ship, afraid someone would discover I wasn't a man. You fought with Flint because of how he lied to me and you've killed Bung all on my account. How much more trouble can I be worth?'

Clay grew serious. 'I think you would be worth dying for, little britches.'

The solemn declaration caused Billy Jo to catch in her breath. She stared at him agape, as if she could not believe her own ears.

'You're a very special girl,' Clay continued in a gentle tone of voice. 'Once you grow up, you're going to be a very fine young lady.'

The surprise vanished from her expression, replaced by a grim determination. 'I'm not a child!'

'No, but you're not a woman yet either.'

'Oh, yeah!' she fired back. 'You think not?'

Clay met the heat in her stare with a mild amusement. 'It won't be long,' he said casually. 'In another year or two you might–'

'Might what?' she jumped in. 'Might learn how to tease a man?' Her tone grew harsh. 'Maybe I can even kiss and cuddle with a few more like Flint! Will that make me a woman?'

A knot of jealousy formed within Clay's chest. 'Those things don't make a woman.'

'Says you!' she scathed him with her words, 'Just what makes you such an expert about women anyhow?'

'Only a complete idiot would claim to be an expert on women!' Clay admitted.

'Then tell me, Mr Valenteen,' she baited him, 'what do I have to do to become a woman?'

Clay groaned inwardly. How had he gotten into this mess? 'I was only trying to–'

'Maybe you could show me?' she continued to goad him. 'What would it take for you to stop calling me little britches and start calling me Billy Jo or miss?'

'If the name bothers you, I can–'

'You're the only one who thinks I'm not a woman yet,' she cut him short a second time. 'Well, I can be as much a woman as any other female in this town.'

'Look, miss ... Billy Jo, I didn't mean to set you off on a ranting session. I was only trying to point out that you've got a lot to learn about living yet. You said it yourself, you've been a slave and prisoner most of your life. How are you supposed to know what real life is all about?'

The logic did not pacify her in the least. She bore into him with eyes as piercing as twin diamond shards.

'I barely remember my folks, but I know what love is, Mr Valenteen. More than that, I know what it is I want.'

He gave a sigh of resignation. 'And what is that, Billy Jo?'

Clay had been sucker punched a time or two. He'd been ambushed more than once and even woke up one time to discover a bear cub standing with its nose inches from his own. He'd been shocked, surprised and occasionally victimized. Still, he didn't see it coming–

Billy Jo leaned over and planted her mouth on his. Both of her hands went up behind his head and she drew him forward, kissing him soundly on the lips. She held him there, a helpless captive to her wiles.

Clay was so dumbfounded, he did nothing

but enjoy the blissful few seconds. When Billy Jo broke away, he sat numbly, staring at her in awe.

'So,' she challenged breathlessly, 'is that the kiss of a child or a woman?'

He maladroitly swallowed his surprise and cleared his throat. 'I stand corrected,' Clay said compliantly. 'I've never been kissed like that before, not by any kind of woman!'

The remark caused Billy Jo to duck her head demurely, obviously embarrassed at having been so impetuous. Even so, she did not back down.

'I keep telling you, I'm eighteen years old,' she murmured. 'I wanted to remove any doubts that I'm still a child.'

'You sure enough proved your point, ma'am,' Clay agreed.

She lifted her eyes, but the reddish hue from her chagrin remained about her cheeks. 'I know a girl is supposed to let the man do the kissin' and courtin', but–'

'Don't apologize for giving me the best kiss of my life.'

'Yes, but I shouldn't have...' She hesitated, shielding her eyes with her lids. 'I mean, it wasn't proper of me to ... to...'

Rather than force her to languish in mortification, Clay put a hand under her chin and lifted her head. At the same time, he leaned over and placed a gentle kiss on her lips. He didn't linger, pulling back after a brief contact.

'That's how our first kiss should have been,' he said. 'And it's something I have wanted to do since I first discovered you were not a boy.'

'Really?' she asked, wholly innocent.

'Even though Flint is a womanizing maggot, I can't blame him for choosing to try and court you, Billy Jo. You are a very special young lady indeed.'

Finally, a smile came to her lips. 'I must admit you did a fair job of defending my honor with him. When I happened to meet him on the street, he about knocked two men down trying to put some distance between us.'

'Man isn't as dumb as I first thought.'

'So, what is your plan now?' she asked.

Clay put on a thoughtful expression. 'I figure I might say something sweet and flowery, offer to buy you supper later and maybe earn myself another kiss.'

Billy Jo laughed. 'You know what I meant. What about the guns and your partner?'

'Oh, them!' he said, as if he had forgotten all about his present situation.

'Yes, what about them?'

Clay suppressed the notion of further romance and returned to business. 'You need to continue with your catalog sales here in town. I'll keep on renting a horse to ride out to the nearby ranches or farms. The travel gives me a cover for sneaking back to the edge of town and watching for the wagon. I have to be ready to follow Grady and whoever else goes to deliver the guns.'

'What about help?' she asked. 'You can't arrest a dozen men all by yourselves.'

'I might need you to lend a hand on that count.'

'Anything,' she volunteered.

'Before we get in to the details, there's one other thing we need to do.' At her curious look, he went on, 'We need to buy you a second dress, some new shoes and a few other necessities.' He felt a lightness in his chest at the bright twinkle that entered her eyes, like tiny sparkles of light dancing about madly. 'Can't have my ward looking like she stole her clothes from a beggar.'

'Mr Valenteen, I–'

'Clay,' he corrected. 'Call me Clay.'

Instead of making a fuss or arguing, she smiled. 'I happened to notice a pretty pink dress over at the general store. It's a bit more fancy than a plain house dress, but it would do me just fine.'

'After we visit the telegraph office to make certain Judge Stickley sent that wire, we're going to do some shopping,' Clay said. 'Next we'll get a second room at the hotel. We can't keep trying to use the same bed at different hours.'

'Whatever you say, Clay,' she said with a smile. 'After all, you're my guardian.'

Flint was supposed to have been keeping an eye on the drummer, but he had lost track of him when he went to speak to Locke. He spotted Valenteen as he escorted Billy Jo over to the general store. They remained inside for some time. When they returned to the street, she had a bundle in her arms and was smiling and laughing.

Damn, she's a whole lot prettier than I remembered!

He watched the couple and felt the sting of envy.

She ought to be hanging on my arm, not hitched up with a blasted salesman! I'm the reason she ran away and came to Yuma! I'm the one she should be laughing and smiling at.

Lotty assailed his thoughts like a dark cloud. He cringed, thinking of her green-eyed jealousy and the cool disdain in her voice. He remembered the grip of her long-nailed fingers digging into his arm each time she cussed at him for looking at another woman. He had put up with her dominating ways, her short temper and icy stares for nearly two years. She ruled over him like a tyrant. He was a slave, a serf, subject to her beck and call.

He wished he could be rid of her, but it was her house they shared and he often needed her help with finances. Every time he got paid, he lost his money gambling, or spent it on drink and good times. He needed Lotty, but she had grown weary of his wandering eye. She had warned him, after Billy Jo arrived, that this had better be the last girl to come looking for him. If it happened again, she would kick him out.

He sighed. Without that interfering woman, things could sure have been different between him and Billy Jo. When she arrived in town, he could have enjoyed having her fawn over him and yield to his desires. He would have kept her around until he grew tired of her. Seeing her in a dress, formfitting enough to accent her youthful, womanly features, he knew he had missed out on a great opportunity.

He watched the girl and Valenteen enter the hotel together. Billy Jo clung to his arm as if fearful a wind would blow her away. *Dag-nab-it!* If not for that drummer, he might have figured a way to have some fun with the girl. He wanted revenge against the salesman, but knew better than to tackle him in any kind of fair fight. His ribs were sore and a couple of his teeth were still loose from the power of the man's punches. With a gun, Bung had been the king of the territory. He was faster than anyone Flint had ever seen, yet Valenteen had taken him in a fair fight.

Flint began to roll himself a smoke, while pondering his misfortune and missed opportunities. Valenteen had moved in and taken up with his girl and beat him senseless in public too. There had to be a safe way to even the score, but how to do it? Word would spread about Valenteen's prowess with both his fists and guns. That meant there wouldn't be a man within a hundred miles who would risk going up against him.

A thought struck home.

That's it! He thought jubilantly. It doesn't have to be someone from around Yuma, it needs to be someone who wants something for themselves ... and he knew who that someone would be. Walking toward the telegraph office, it hurt to smile, but he withstood the pain without complaint.

CHAPTER SEVEN

Clay left Billy Jo at the hotel. She wanted to take a bath before putting on her new clothes. Meanwhile, he decided to check in with the marshal. Baxter seemed an honest sort and everyone who spoke of him did so with an amount of respect. If he was in Locke's pocket, he had covered his tracks nicely around town.

Baxter was on the working end of a broom, sweeping out the jail when Clay arrived. The man stopped his labor and offered up a smile of greeting.

'Trouble with not having anyone locked up,' he explained with a grin, 'there's no one to do the cleaning but me.'

Clay got right to the point. 'You strike me as an intelligent and able man, Marshal. How did you wind up in Yuma?'

'Same story as a good many men out in these parts, Valenteen. I wandered most of

132

my youth away looking for gold, hiring on for a trail drive, or spending the winter holed up in some dirt-water town tending bar. Even did some trapping for a time, but didn't care for the solitude. I also worked on a steamship, much like the one you rode coming here, but the infernal heat was more than I could stand.'

Clay chuckled. 'You don't like heat so you put down roots here?'

'You were on the river,' Baxter pointed out. 'A hundred degrees in the shade is not nearly as hot as eighty degrees on the water.'

'The river does seem to multiply the heat all right.'

'Actually, I landed this job by chance,' the marshal explained. 'I was having a beer at the saloon when a couple rowdies got into a fight. They were busting up the place and I stepped in and put an end to the brawl.'

'How so?'

'Clubbed one on the knee and the other over the head. The barkeep helped me drag them down to the jail, but there wasn't anyone to watch over them. I stayed the night and herded them before Stickley to pay for damages. He offered me the job. I get room and board, a small salary and a share of any fines imposed.'

'What is the story about the judge? Funny to find a man educated in the law way out here too.'

Baxter rubbed the rough stubble on his jaw. 'Must be getting old,' he muttered. 'I plum forgot to shave today.'

Clay didn't respond to his observation and the marshal got around to his question. 'From what I've learned, Stickley arrived here shortly after the Union won the war over the Confederate States. He took on being mayor, petitioned the territorial governor and was appointed judge. I don't know much more, except he seems to have enough money to get by comfortably.'

'And Locke?'

The question put a curious look on Baxter's face. 'You sure ask a lot of questions.'

'I have cause to wonder and maybe worry some,' Clay said, 'being that I killed two of Locke's men.'

'He has a few hired men for his storage and transfer business, shipping goods and supplies to nearby ranches or settlements. He also hired a young couple to run his store.'

'Any idea if Locke might have sent Bung after me?'

'I thought he was out to collect the reward being offered for the girl?'

'Probably, Marshal, but I like to cover all of the options. If Locke is out to get me, I could end up dead real sudden. I'd like to know more about him.'

'Seems Locke arrived a few months after Stickley. I wasn't here at the time, but Benny, who runs the livery, once told me he come here with only the clothes on his back. If so, he's done himself proud building up the business at his general store like he has.'

'If he was broke, how did he manage to build and supply a store?'

'I suppose he borrowed the money; I really couldn't say.'

'Maybe he was engaged in something illegal?'

At Baxter's frown, Clay knew he had given himself away. The marshal was no fool.

'All right, Valenteen,' he said, 'let's cut the rope and turn the bull loose. You don't talk like a salesman, you ask questions like a lawman or investigator of some kind. Who are you?'

'Maybe I'm just nosy.'

'And maybe Lard Ackers did catch you snooping in that cargo hold.'

Clay stuck to his own questions.

'There's still a lot of Indian trouble up this way. Most of the Comanche and Apache have been moved to reservations, other than the band led by Chappabitty.'

'Chappabitty has his mind set to be as revered as Cochise or Geronimo,' Baxter said. 'I recall the tale of him being a *working captive* in his youth.' With a snort, 'Leastways that's what civilized folks call it. Sounds better than referring to their Indian servants or workers as slaves.' He got back to the point. 'The thing is, if Knocks-Enemy-from-his-Horse gets enough followers, he is going to make a lot of trouble. So far, his raids have mostly been against small farms or ranches or an occasional unprotected wagon. It only takes a couple of men with rifles to keep his raiders at bay.' Baxter snorted. 'Not exactly the kind of reputation that encourages other braves to join his fight.'

'If Chappabitty managed to get his hands on some of the new Model '73 Winchester rifles, he would certainly attract new followers.'

Baxter frowned. 'You're talking about a traitor dealing rifles to the Indians.'

It was not a question, but Clay gave an affirmative nod. 'I've been following a shipment of stolen guns since they were taken from a railroad car. They are here in Yuma.'

'I commence to see you are going to cause

me a mountain of trouble, son,' Baxter said. 'Considering the questions you been asking, you think Locke is involved.'

'The guns are in his warehouse and Lard Ackers worked for him.'

'As did Bung,' Baxter added, 'and both men tried to kill you.'

'Which probably means they suspect me. I know I've been followed and watched since I arrived. It was Bung at the beginning, but now I believe Flint is my shadow.'

'Question is,' Baxter said, lifting a guarded eyebrow, 'why come to me?'

'I'm taking a chance that you're an honest man.'

'Betting your life on it would be more accurate.'

Clay continued to evaluate the marshal. He had to trust his instincts and hope the man was honest. With a wry grin he laid his cards on the table.

'Once the gun runners make their move, I'm going to need some help arresting them. I would appreciate your help.'

'How many men are we talking about?'

'Don't have a clue,' Clay answered truthfully. I doubt Locke deals with Chappabitty directly. I figure there is a middleman who will meet the wagon and pick up the guns. I intend to grab everyone involved at the meeting place, but I can't very well arrest a half-dozen men all by myself.'

'Ain't much of a lawman, are you?' Baxter quipped. 'I once heard of a Texas Ranger who arrested Bloody Dave Banks and a gang of fifteen cut-throat renegades all by himself.'

'First time I heard that story it was Dave and three poorly armed renegades, and the ranger had a ten-man posse with him.'

Baxter laughed. 'I reckon the tale has been – what's the term? – *embellished* over time.'

'Seriously, Marshal, can I count on you to lend a hand?'

'I'd about do anything to put an end to the Indian raids,' Baxter replied.

'How many trustworthy men can you raise in a short span of time, say ten to fifteen minutes?'

Two distinct lines furrowed the marshal's brow as he did some quick thinking. 'Three, maybe four. Given more time I could round up a dozen or more.'

'There won't be time, Marshal. When I send word for help, the wagon will already be under way. You will have to gather men and catch up in order to save me from getting shot full of holes.'

'Seems to me this plan of yours might have

some holes in it, too,' Baxter said. 'If you get killed, I won't have a notion in Hades what to do about it or who to contact.'

'Let's not let it get that far out of hand.'

'Easy enough said, but–'

'It's the way it has to be.' Clay prevented further discussion. 'We can't move until we can grab the go-between, the one linking Locke and the Indians. Once he is out in the open, we can stop the transfer of weapons and make the arrests.'

'All right, Valenteen, count me in. When you say the word, I'll round up men I can trust and come a running.'

Clay stuck out his hand. 'Thanks, Marshal, I really appreciate this.'

'Some of the recent Indian raids have been right close to here, kilt a few people I knew and liked. I'm the one who should be thanking you.'

'If we get through this all right, we can buy each other a drink to celebrate.'

Baxter grinned. 'And if we both end up dead, then who the hell cares?'

Clay sat in at a card game for the next hour. He chose a chair where he could watch Locke's storehouse. By dusk, nothing had moved so he cashed in his chips and returned to the hotel.

He arrived at the door to his room and a girl stepped out into the hallway. He paused in mid-reach for the knob, struck by the loveliness of the young woman. Her hair was fairly short but set off her angelic face like a picture frame. Dark lashes decorated her rich, chocolate-colored eyes and her ripe, full lips beckoned to be kissed. The dress fitted snug at the waist and bosom, while the flowing skirt rode an inch above the floor, revealing a portion of her new shoes.

'I was beginning to wonder if you were ever coming back to the hotel,' Billy Jo said softly. 'Did you run into more trouble?'

'Whoa!' Clay exclaimed. 'Is that you, Billy Jo?'

'Of course it's me,' she said, frowning at his antics. 'Who were you expecting?'

'A young girl ... one who passed herself off as a boy,' he stammered. 'But you? Danged if you aren't about the most beautiful creature I ever seen!'

The praise brought a hint of color to her cheeks, but she smiled at the praise. 'I never did have much chance to dress up proper like,' she told him. 'I didn't want Jonas or his boys to be looking at me. This here is the first new dress I've ever had.'

'Well, let me tell you, gal, you make one heck of a woman.'

She laughed, but her eyes were filled with a rare delight. 'I never thought of you as a man so full of flattery, Clay. Where you been hiding your manners all this time?'

'I must have lost them for a spell. Seeing you now I can't imagine how I ever mistook you for a boy.'

'Is the marshal going to help?' she asked, turning to business.

'He says he can get three or four men at a moment's notice.'

Billy Jo became serious. 'Is that going to be enough? What if the Indians show up at the meeting place? You can't take on a bunch of savages and Locke's men by yourself.'

'I don't think Locke would risk being linked that closely to the Indians. I'm betting there is a middleman, one who deals with both Locke and the Indians. He's the one we have to catch. Greedy bloodsuckers like Locke betray their countrymen for money, but they need a way to contact the enemy. That's where the middleman comes in. He'll be the one who knows how to deal with the Indians. We take him out, we break the chain.'

'What now?'

Clay reached out and took hold of the girl's hand. 'Now we go get something to eat and I suffer the envy of every man in town.'

The words brought forth a coy lowering of her eyes, but Billy Jo moved up to lace her arm through his. As they started off down the hall, she emitted a soft laugh.

'That first day, when we were hauled off of the steamship in chains, I never thought we would end up having dinner together like we was courting.'

'That goes double for me,' Clay replied. 'After all, I still thought you were a boy.'

Billy Jo laughed. Clay smiled, enjoying the sound of her mirth, until he spied the clerk at the counter. The man lifted a piece of paper.

'Message for you, Mr Valenteen,' he announced. 'A town runner brought it by not more than five minutes ago.'

Clay moved over and took the page. To reward the clerk for his courtesy and for providing Billy Jo with a bath, Clay dropped a silver dollar on the counter.

'Thank you, Mr Valenteen,' the clerk said with a smile. 'Anything else you need while you're here, you only have to ask.'

Clay gave him a nod and returned to Billy Jo's side. She looked over at the paper and then put a curious look on him.

'What is the message about?' she asked.

Clay read the note aloud. 'Want to order one of those J.B. Stetson hats before you leave town. I'll be gone tomorrow morning, but will get you the money before dark. Thanks. G.M. Hennesy.'

He tucked the sheet of paper in his pocket as they left the hotel.

'Who is Mr Hennesy?' Billy Jo asked. 'One of the customers you spoke with?'

'It's from Grady,' Clay told her in a hushed voice. 'The guns are being taken out in the morning. Far as he knows, it's maybe half a day's ride.'

'Because he says he will be back before dark,' the girl reasoned.

'Yes. I will need to figure a way to get out of town without Flint knowing about it.'

'How can you do that?' Billy Jo asked. 'He's been dogging us ever since you killed Bung.'

Clay thought for a moment and then smiled. 'I think I've got a plan that might work.' He winked at her. 'That is, with your help.'

Flint rubbed the sleep out of his eyes and yawned. A two-hour nap would have to hold him for the rest of the night. Rather than go relieve the night guard at the storehouse, he went the opposite direction and found Mort, watching the hotel, sitting on an empty flour barrel and smoking a cigarette.

'Anything going on, Mort?'

'Drummer and the girl returned to the hotel a couple hours after dark. I ain't seen hide nor hair of either one since.'

'You staying here for a bit longer?'

'No need,' he answered. 'You'll be guarding the warehouse. If he comes snooping, you put a bullet in him. That would settle everyone's nerves.'

'Bung tried that and it didn't work out too well,' Flint retorted.

Mort snorted his agreement and said, 'Tell you one thing, pard, I'm glad we're getting rid of those guns tomorrow. Watching some salesman night and day is not my idea of a fun job.'

'Yeah, tell me about it,' Flint replied. 'I've had to follow him out to a number of farms and ranches. Talk about a hot, miserable chore, sitting in the sun, while he is invited inside a house for shade and a cool drink.'

'You ain't coming tomorrow?'

'I'm hoping to catch a few winks tonight while on guard. Henry and Grady are your pals for tomorrow's run. When you pull out, I'll be squatting right here, watching for Valenteen to make one wrong move. If he decides to ride out as usual, I'll be on his trail.'

Mort stretched out his arms. 'It's the bunk for me. Be a long day tomorrow. We'll load up at first light and meet Banty at the usual place about noon.'

'You don't have to worry about the drummer,' Flint told him firmly. 'If he makes a turn in your direction, I'll see that he has himself a fatal accident.'

Mort gave a bob of his head and started up the street. 'See you later.'

Flint called a reply and started up the street for the storehouse. It was going to be a long night.

As daylight spread to encompass the world, Flint returned to keep watch across from the hotel. His eyes burned for want of sleep, but he took solace in that this was the last day they would be watching Valenteen. Once the rifles were delivered, their worries about the salesman were over.

Flint slumped down on the same flour barrel Mort had used the previous night and leaned back against the wall of the building. It was peaceful and quiet as the sun began to break over the eastern horizon. Flint had to fight off the drowsy effects of being up all night. To try and stay alert, he removed a small wad of paper and tobacco sack from his shirt pocket. Before he could roll himself a cigarette, he spotted Billy Jo.

He sat up straight as she stopped on the walk in front of the hotel and looked up and down the street. When she spied him, she made a direct line in his direction.

'What the hell?' Flint muttered, shoving the cigarette makings back into his shirt pocket.

Billy Jo did not alter her course walking over to him deliberately.

'I need to speak to you, Flint,' she said crisply.

Flint flashed a hurried glance past her, watching the front of the hotel. Billy Jo moved off to the alleyway, as if not wanting to be seen from the hotel.

'What's this about, kid?' he asked.

'It's important.'

Flint gulped down his surprise and rose up from his makeshift stool. As he followed after Billy Jo, she about took his breath away. Decked out in her pretty new dress, with her hair curled to accent the delicate features of her angelic face, she looked like a princess from a fairy-story.

'I – I'm kind of busy, honeycomb,' he stammered, desperately trying to keep his mind on business. 'Maybe we can get together later.'

'That woman you are staying with,' Billy Jo challenged. 'Do you prefer her to me?'

Flint was stunned. 'I thought you had taken up with the drummer?'

'That snake is worse than you, Flint!' she fumed. 'He has a wife and two kids!'

The news shocked Flint to his boot heels. 'You're funning me!'

'That sneaky, no good womanizer,' she grated the words. 'He tells me I'm beautiful and buys me new clothes. He gives me a job to help me get on my feet. Then he takes me out to dinner as if I'm his best girl.' Billy Jo folded her arms and stomped a few steps further down the alley. Flint followed along until she stopped suddenly and whirled about to face him again.

'Want to know what he had in mind after dinner?' she asked vehemently.

He mustered an indignant scowl. 'You don't mean he got ... familiar?'

'Familiar!' she exploded, balling her small hands into fists. 'He wanted for us to share the same room! He expected payment for being nice to me!'

'The miserable cur!' he hissed the words. 'I can't believe a man would stoop so low.'

'What about it?' Billy Jo ranted. 'Do you fancy the woman you live with over me?'

Flint was dumbfounded by the question. He sized up the situation and it wasn't pretty. This girl appeared to have a purpose in mind. He had seen the look before, the wild eyes, the firm set of the jaw, the grim determination. She was thinking matrimony!

'Uh, well...' – his mind worked at triple speed – 'it's like this, honeycomb. I ain't as dishonest as the drummer. I would never make the vows to one woman, 'cause I know I couldn't be faithful. You know what I mean?'

Billy Jo took a menacing step toward him. 'You kissed me and said you wanted to take care of me!' she reminded him. 'Didn't those words mean anything?'

'Pull in the reins and listen, little lady,' Flint back-pedaled. 'I was only talking; I never made any promises.'

'You asked me to come to Yuma!' Billy Jo fired back. 'You said we could be together!'

'Yeah, but I didn't think you'd really come all this way.'

'Are all men the same?' she scathed him with her attack. 'Are you no better than a bunch of hounds around a female dog in season?'

'It's not like that at all,' Flint whined, lifting his hands, palms outward to ward her off. 'You're making a full-growed tree out of a single acorn. There's more to life than getting married and having a bunch of snotty-nosed kids running around the house. A person ought to have some fun first, you know, just a little harmless fun.'

Billy Jo glowered at him. 'So I'm supposed to be more like you – a free spirit, a woman without morals or conscience, who surrenders her virtue to the first scoundrel who asks.'

'Damn, girl,' Flint carped, 'you make it sound down right despicable.'

'It is despicable!' she cried. 'And so are you!'

Flint opened his mouth, trying to find words to soothe the woman's ire, but she side-stepped him, stormed up the alley and back across the street. When she reached the hotel, she went inside and never looked back.

'Whoa!' Flint muttered aloud, finally able to take a breath. 'And I thought Lotty had a temper!'

Clay quickly saddled his horse and made his way around to the side of the barn. He took a peek down the street in time to see Billy Jo cross back to the hotel. Flint was at the edge of the street staring after her with a bewildered look on his face. The little gal had done a good job of keeping the man's attention. He had not seen Clay slip away and it would be some time before he would get curious enough to actually go into the hotel looking for him. By then it would be too late.

Clay mounted up and left town by a back street. He circled to a knobby hill, rode up to the summit and tethered his horse on a stout piece of rope. From his vantage point he could see both ends of the main street. Whichever way the wagon went, he would see it.

Thirty minutes passed before the wagon appeared. There were two outriders, Mort Lindsay and the usual night guard from the warehouse. Grady was driving the rig, his hat pulled low to shield his eyes from the morning sun.

'The time has come,' he said. 'Billy Jo, honey, I sure hope you're keeping a sharp eye.'

He scraped together several bits of wood and used a match to start a small fire. Once the few sticks were burning, he dropped in the grease-soaked rag he had scrounged at the livery. As the material began to burn, it put off a dirty grey smoke. With nary a breeze, the smoke rose straight up into the clear sky.

Using his ground blanket, he covered the fire for a second, interrupting the smoke. He pulled it back quickly to allow the smoke to resume its upward course. After a full five seconds he repeated the process. Two puffs of smoke for south. Finished relaying the direction of the wagon, he kicked out the fire and grabbed up his horse. Within moments, he was on the move.

Flint was growing restless. Valenteen should have put in an appearance by this time. He usually got a quick start in the mornings to beat the heat. His concern doubled when he spotted Billy Jo again. She did not look his direction this time, but turned up the street. She seemed to be walking with intent, so Flint moved along the opposite walk and kept her in sight. When she entered the jail, he came to a sudden stop.

A gnawing in his gut told him something was not right. Why would Billy Jo go to see Baxter? Was she going to report what Valenteen had tried? Did she think she could press charges against the drummer?

That didn't ring true. In fact, after pondering on it some, nothing she had done this morning made any sense. She had made it clear she wanted nothing more to do with him, then she had approached him and told him about Valenteen. She next suggested she would be willing to renew their relationship by asking if he preferred Lotty over her. Before he had managed a suitable answer, she had blown up and started yapping like a stepped on pup. He was left trying to figure out what game she was playing while she stormed off to the hotel.

'So what is really going on?' he wondered aloud.

Baxter suddenly appeared at the doorway. Flint ducked down an alley quickly so he would not be seen. After a few seconds, he peered around the corner of the building to see Baxter speaking to Billy Jo. He seemed in a hurry, talking at her over his shoulder. Flint strained to hear what was being said.

'...don't worry about a thing,' were his last words. A warning bell began to chime in Flint's head, ringing like the church tower before Sunday service. Something was wrong. Something was very wrong!

Rather than keep watch for Valenteen, Flint shadowed Baxter down the street. The marshal rushed through the tanning-shop door, exited a moment later and walked brusquely to the barber shop. Before he left there the barber had placed a 'Closed' sign in the window.

Flint's heart began to pound. The wagon-load of guns would have left by this time. If Valenteen was involved, he must have managed to sneak out of town without Flint seeing him. He was probably following the wagon at this very moment. The only possible deduction sent a chill of fear surging through Flint. Whether Valenteen was a government agent or lawman – *damn!* even if he was not involved in any way – it no longer mattered: Baxter was gathering a posse!

Moving along a back alley, Flint kept pace with the marshal. His last stop was to visit Judge Stickley. He could be asking for warrants to arrest Locke and all of his men. Baxter came out after a couple minutes and continued along the street. By the time the marshal reached the livery he had three men with him. With his back pressed against the wall of the adjacent building, Flint got as close as he dared and strained to hear what was being said.

'Sure the four of us will be enough?' It was the barber speaking.

'Valenteen didn't think there would be

more than four or five at the meeting site. He will be there to help make the arrests. We should only have to throw down on a couple gun runners who aren't expecting trouble.'

'Be a blessing to stop the Indian attacks,' another man spoke. It sounded like the tinsmith. 'My wife's brother was ambushed just last month. His boy was killed and he still don't walk good from the arrow he caught in the leg.'

'That's why I'm here,' the barber chimed in. 'Lost my uncle last year to renegades. Give those red devils new rifles and it won't be safe for man, woman or child within a hundred miles.'

'Let's stop gabbing and get going,' Baxter said. 'We know to head south and then we'll watch for sign. Valenteen will be counting on us.'

Flint didn't have to hear more. He faded away from the building and hurried off to warn Locke. It was time to get out of Yuma!

CHAPTER EIGHT

Clay kept the wagon in sight, but remained far enough back that he wouldn't be seen. After five or six miles the wagon left the main road to follow a faint trail toward a few choppy hills. The land was open and offered little cover. Clay left a marker for Baxter and kept a respectful distance between himself and the wagon. If he was spotted, the whole operation would fail.

He wondered how long it would be until Baxter and the posse arrived. He figured to be an hour ahead of them, but they would move much quicker than the wagon. He didn't want them catching up too soon. A lone man on horseback could stay hidden, not so a half-dozen riders.

Keeping just beyond the sight of the wagon, Clay continually swept the horizon, watching for any sign of movement. The gun runners might be careless about their meeting, but he couldn't count on it. One of the outriders hanging back, a lookout for the middleman, one glimpse could ruin his approach and possibly get him and Grady both killed.

The mid-morning heat became sweltering. Clay's shirt grew damp under the arms and down the middle of his back. Heat waves rose from the desert floor like a translucent curtain, blurring and distorting distant images and landmarks. From high overhead a lone hawk glided through the sky, likely seeking cool pockets of air, while scanning the ground below for a meal. Slight clouds of dust rose up from his horse's hoofs to sting Clay's eyes and invade his nostrils. Other than the sound of the animal beneath him and his own breathing, the world was a silent tomb. It appeared that, other than the solitary hawk, not a creature was stirring for as far as the eye could see.

Clay scrutinized the trail and kept moving. He reasoned the middleman would probably take the rifles and ammunition away either by mules or pack horses. Chappabitty's band probably kept to the rugged country, where they could more easily hide and disappear. They avoided the open country where the cavalry could run them to ground. It was likely a wagon could not make such a journey. Yep, everything appeared to be going as planned.

The marshal had told Billy Jo to go back to the hotel and wait, but first she wanted to make sure he had enough men to help Clay. Following after Baxter, she watched him until he and his three-man posse hurried off to the livery. As the four of them were saddling their horses, she caught sight of a shadowy figure in a nearby alley.

The man had obviously been watching the marshal. As he darted down the passageway she recognized Flint. He was moving quickly, making a circle away from the livery, then across the street, working his way back to the general store. He was going to warn Locke!

Billy Jo started toward the livery but was too late. Baxter and the others were already mounted and sped out of town at a gallop, hurrying to catch up with Clay. There was no one to stop Locke and Flint from getting away. By the time Clay and the others returned, the man responsible for trading rifles to the Indians would be long gone.

What to do.

She stared after the posse, anxiously turning over ideas, wondering who she could turn to. Then she remembered Judge Stickley. Baxter had stopped by to see him, probably to let him know what was going on. The judge might have an idea of how to prevent Locke from getting away.

Billy Jo whirled about and walked swiftly up the street to the judge's house. The door was ajar. Perhaps he was in the process of trying to round up a second larger posse. She pushed open the door, stepped inside and opened her mouth to call out his name–

'I warned you about him!' Judge Stickley's voice boomed. 'Damn it all, Locke! You've gone and ruined everything.'

'You can't blame me, Del,' Locke whined. 'I had the man watched around the clock. It ain't my fault.'

'We better grab whatever we can and put some distance between us and Yuma before Valenteen and the marshal get back. You know Henry and Mort will be only too eager to spill their guts and tell everything they know.'

'They don't know about you.'

'Once they take a look into your background they will sure as hell know. A captain and a sergeant from the same Confederate company? How long do you think it will take them to–'

Billy Jo backed up abruptly, shocked at the conversation. In her haste to retreat back through the door she bumped into a third man – Flint.

He caught hold of her arms with his hands and sneered, 'Well, well, honeycomb, what the devil are you doing here?'

Stickley and Locke came from the next room to confront the intruder as one.

'What the hell, Locke?' Stickley boomed. 'Did you announce to the world that we were involved in gun running? Is there anyone in town who doesn't know?'

Locke could only shake his head in wonder.

'What do we do with the brat?' Flint asked. 'She will run to Valenteen as soon as he arrives back in town.'

An icy knot of fear formed in Billy Jo's chest. She held her breath, knowing she was about one whisper from death.

'We could kill her,' Locke suggested grimly.

Stickley discounted that idea. 'Dealing guns to the Indians isn't enough for you, Locke?' he asked sarcastically. 'You want that undercover sneak following you for the rest of your days?'

'He's got it bad for the brat here,' Flint agreed. 'Kill her and he'll follow us into the fires of hell. How about we can tie her up and leave her some place.'

'We sure can't let her run free,' Locke replied. 'If word of us dealing guns to the

Indians got out, there would be a dozen men here to hang us before you could spit.'

'She might be useful,' Stickley suggested. 'We can take her with us. Once we are a day's ride from here, we dump her in the desert to help slow down any pursuit.'

Locke looked at the judge. 'That ain't a bad idea, Del.'

'Especially if she isn't in the best condition for travel,' Stickley added. He gave a nod to Flint. 'Truss her up, stuff a gag in her mouth and stash her where she can't cause any trouble. Gather only what you can carry and plan on some hard travel till we're in the clear. We leave in thirty minutes.'

Flint was stuck with Billy Jo, but needed to pick up his belongings. He bound her hands and stuffed a sock in her mouth, securing it with a strip of cloth. He grinned at her, once she was helpless, and leaned in close enough to kiss her.

'You do as I say, honeycomb, and you can live to share a little cottage with Valenteen and have yourself a half-dozen snotty-nosed kids. You give us any trouble and you'll never see that man again.' He gave his head a tilt to one side, peering into her eyes so she would know he was serious. 'Are you listening?'

Billy Jo could do little more than grunt

through the material, so she gave her head an affirmative nod.

'Good girl,' Flint said. 'I'm going to stick you in the judge's closet, while I sneak over to Lotty's place and get my stuff. If you make so much as a peep, Stickley or Locke will put a bullet in your brain. We're all facing a noose and they can only hang a man once for dealing guns to the Indians. Killing you won't change our fate if we get caught. Do you understand?'

Billy Jo bobbed her head a second time.

Flint led her to a hallway closet and pushed her inside. Stowed in the dark cubicle, with no light and malodorous air, thick with the smell of dust and mold, Billy Jo could only listen to Flint as he blocked the door. She listened to the sound of his boots striking the wooden floor as he left, but the judge was nearby. He would be cleaning out his safe and gathering supplies for the trip. She dared not try getting loose or forcing open the door. The consensus was to take her along and leave her, albeit a bit incapacitated, to slow down pursuit. Her first priority had to be staying alive.

Clay stopped his mount and listened intently. The faint sound of the wagon was no longer audible. He nosed his horse in between two scraggly mesquite bushes and stepped down. He secured his tether rope to the sturdy base of a stout bush and quickly removed his rifle from the boot. Jacking a shell into the chamber, he kept the weapon at the ready, his right hand at the grip, finger alongside the trigger. Then he set off, weaving a silent path for the nearest hillock. He needed to get high enough to have a look at what was going on with the wagon and two outriders.

The sun heated his shoulders and his brow became beaded with sweat. Moving quiet yet steadily, he worked around the side of a hill, keeping below the crest. He was careful not to silhouette himself against the sky and attract any undue attention.

Voices reached his ears and he grew more cautious. Ducking low, he circled the hill until he spied a slight hollow below. There were three men on horseback – no, make that four.

Grady was atop the wagon seat. He appeared to be completely relaxed, without a care in the world. He had rolled a smoke and the cigarette dangled from the corner of his mouth. To the casual observer he appeared harmless.

Clay knew better. The man he had partnered with several times was alert and ready to act. He lounged with one leg up on the front edge of the wagon and his hat was tipped low on his head. Clay observed how his position allowed him to place his right hand on the butt of his pistol, while the hat would keep the sun's glare from interfering with his target. Grady was set.

Moving to a practical vantage point, Clay located a bit of cover behind a stony mound. He took a last look for the posse. They should be close, but they were going to be too slow. The transfer of rifles was nearly done. He couldn't allow the middleman to escape. He sank to his knees and aligned the rifle, sighting in the nearest of the four men.

'It's the law!' He called out. 'You are surrounded!'

He might as well have shouted to the four men to grab their guns and try to bolt with their horses. That's exactly what they did.

Grady was quick. He drew his gun and fired, striking Mort before he could bring his gun to bear on Clay's position. Henry's usual job was to guard a storehouse, not jump into a gunfight. He immediately threw his hands in the air.

Clay didn't know the other two men, but

one tried to grab iron; he pulled the trigger on his rifle and knocked him out of the saddle. The fourth man turned his horse to make a run, but the posse came thundering up the trail and blocked his escape. He quickly raised his hands to keep from being shot from the saddle.

It all happened in a span of several seconds. Two men were down and the other two were captured. The fourth man could have gotten away from Clay, but the posse had arrived in time to nab him. The short fight was over.

'Sonuvabee! They got us, Banty,' Henry complained to the other mounted rider. 'That damn Locke sent us riding right into a trap!'

'If I get the chance,' the one called Banty vowed, 'I'll sure enough kill Flint, cousin or no.'

With the posse and Grady handling the prisoners, Clay hurried back to pick up his horse and rode down to join Baxter and the others.

'The two on the ground won't be swinging from no rope,' Grady informed him, having inspected both bodies. 'I knew my man was done, but didn't know if you had hit your target square or not. Sometimes you don't shoot worth shucks.'

'You best get your eyes checked,' Clay replied. 'I'm a better shot with a long gun than you are with a pistol.'

Grady uttered a grunt. 'If my eyes are so poor, you're lucky I didn't shoot you by mistake.'

'I'll be sure and remember that for any future gunfights,' Clay quipped. 'Hate to have you kill me by mistake.'

Grady grinned. 'Me too, 'cause I sure couldn't write it up in my report to the captain that way. If it became known that I killed my own partner, no one would work with me again.'

Clay smiled at his humor.

'Good work, you two,' Baxter told them. 'Your stolen rifles won't be helping to kill any settlers.'

'Let's load the bodies and get these guns back to town,' Clay replied. 'I want to see the look on Flint and Locke's face when we put them behind bars with their pals.'

Baxter grinned as well. 'I'm looking forward to that myself.'

Flint had the reins to Billy Jo's horse, as her hands were tied behind her back. She hadn't done much riding and she was feeling the effects after a couple hours in the saddle. The stirrups rubbed against the inside of her legs, her lower torso and back ached from sitting astraddle and the sun burned her exposed face and arms.

'This ought to be far enough,' Locke spoke to Stickley. 'There has been considerable traffic along this part of the trail. It will be some time before the posse figures out we have turned toward Mexico.'

Stickley grunted his assent. 'You always were a wily hound, Locke.'

Locke grinned. 'That's why the army never caught up with us after the war, Del.'

Flint overheard the exchange. 'That's where you two met, during the war?'

Stickley cocked his head at Locke. 'Captain Del Stewart and Sergeant Warren Lannigan of the Confederate Army.' He laughed. 'Well, we started out as part of the Confederacy.'

'Until it became clear who was going to win the war,' Locke explained.

'We rode together for three years until we had to split up when some Yankees were hot on our trail,' Stickley continued. 'I happened on to a Southern gent, a banker, who had just cleaned out his own bank.' Stickley displayed a smirk. 'I decided the army life was not my calling.'

'That's where you got your money,' Flint made the statement.

'Once I settled in Yuma I got word to Locke. He came to work for me and we've been planning a Mexico retirement for the past couple years.'

'Everything was working pretty much to plan until that damned salesman, or who-ever he is, showed up,' Locke said.

Stickley averted his attention, regarding Billy Jo with a hard stare. 'I'm betting you know the truth about the drummer, don't you, my sweet?'

Billy Jo compressed her lips and said nothing.

'Makes no difference,' Stickley dismissed her stubborn disposition. 'We've severed our ties and won't be going back to Yuma.'

'There's the rocky stretch just ahead,' Locke informed him. 'I've been down this road a few times and spotted it as the best place to lose a posse.'

Flint paused to take a drink from his canteen. Surprisingly, he allowed Billy Jo to have a couple of sips of water. She didn't thank him, but it did help to ease the dry-ness of her throat.

Stickley and Locke turned off the main road, riding single file to hide their tracks.

Flint gave Billy Jo an apologetic look. 'Sorry about this, honeycomb,' he said softly, so as to not have the other men hear. 'I didn't mean for you to get mixed up with something like this.'

'Valenteen will hunt you down,' she vowed. 'You can't run from a man like him.'

'Your concern should be about staying alive,' Flint told her. 'You best hope your sweetheart managed to find our trail.'

CHAPTER NINE

Baxter herded Banty and Henry into the jail. The bodies of the two dead men were laid out at the carpenter's place so he could construct their final wooden domiciles.

Clay and Grady went to Locke's store and learned he had picked up some supplies and left without a word of explanation. After a quick search of town, they discovered both Locke and Flint were missing.

The marshal met them in front of the saloon. He looked worried.

'Old Benny, who runs the stable, says the judge and Locke packed up some gear and left right sudden. They took along two extra horses.'

'The judge?' Grady repeated. 'What does he have to do with the gun running?'

'He and Locke,' Baxter muttered. 'They were partners in crime.'

'Good thing we didn't tell him ahead of time about the rifles,' Clay said. 'He could have warned Locke and we would never have captured Banty.'

Baxter groaned. 'I'm afraid I did tell him about the posse. I thought we ought to have someone more official than me involved. Little did I know.'

'So he warned Locke and Flint so the three of them could escape.'

'There's something worse than having the three of them gone missing,' the barber said, having just come back from putting up his horse. 'My wife saw Flint and Billy Jo leave town, too. She said the four of them left by the back streets and were headed northeast toward Phoenix.'

'Think they might have friends up that way?' Grady asked the marshal.

'I don't know, Grady. I'll have a posse together and be ready to ride in about fifteen minutes. We need to catch them before they reach Phoenix.'

Clay watched the marshal hurry out the door. He waved to a man to join him and they both rushed into the general store, probably to pick up some supplies.

Grady looked at Clay. 'What do you think?'

'I have to wonder at their direction.'

'They could have friends in Phoenix,' Grady offered. 'Maybe they have an escape route all laid out. With a few hours' head start, we might never catch up with them.'

'You take charge of the rifles. I'll get a few things together for a hard ride.'

'The barber is sure enough honest. I'll leave the rifles with him or his wife until we get back.'

Clay agreed and parted company with Grady. He went to his hotel room to gather his traveling gear. He was in the midst of stuffing clothes into his war bag when his door opened. The woman standing there was not familiar to him, but she wore a stern expression. Little of her youth remained in her face and what there was had been covered with powder and rouge.

'I'm Lotty,' she explained, 'Flint Cooner's lady friend.'

Clay politely tipped his hat. 'Proud to meet you, ma'am. What can I do for you?'

The lines at the corner of her mouth lifted

with a slight amusement at his courtesy. 'Flint took off with Locke and your young lady friend,' she replied in a matter-of-fact tone of voice. 'He said they were going to make a fake trail for Phoenix, but they are really headed for Mexico.'

'How do you know this?'

She made an unladylike snort. 'I caught him packing his things. He never had much backbone, but he was company.' She waved a hand, as if brushing away a fly. 'I've lived with that snake for two years. Guess I know when he's telling me the truth or not. He told me he would send for me. I know he was lying, but he was plenty serious about crossing the border.'

'Why would you tell me which way he's going.'

'Because that miserable drunken oaf took that farm girl with him. I ain't gonna' sit here watching the wood splinter while he is off fondling and kissing some half-grown nymph!' Her ire caused color to flush her cheeks and two veins stood out against her forehead. 'I warned him not to leave me behind, but he was too blamed loco in the head about that flashy little witch. He aims to take her for his own self.'

'Not if I catch up to him,' Clay vowed.

'That's why I'm telling you,' she admitted. 'Alley cat that he is I'll wait for him to serve a couple of years of busting rock. He never kilt no one and never went to exchange any guns. He has always been little more than a town runner for Locke. I don't figure he will get more than a year or two behind bars for that.'

Clay didn't bother to tell her that he was liable to be charged with kidnapping too. If so, he would be behind prison walls for the rest of his life.

'I appreciate your coming to me,' he told Lotty. 'I'll do what I can to see that no harm comes to Flint.'

The woman gave a bob of her head and backed out of the room. Without another word she closed the door and Clay heard her steps going down the hallway. She was some woman, willing to help her man get caught so he wouldn't run out on her. Maybe she figured after Flint did his jail time he would make a better husband.

Clay buckled up the war bag and headed out the door. The sun would be setting soon and Flint and the others would probably ride well into the night. There was no time to waste.

The small party stopped sometime after midnight to rest the horses and get a couple of hours' sleep. Billy Jo ached all over. She was stiff from the small of her back up into her shoulders and suffered from the fiery sensation caused by the saddle fenders rubbing the hide raw along the insides of her legs. Add a dose of sunburn and having her wrists bound and she didn't figure to get much rest.

It seemed she had finally slipped into an exhausted slumber when she heard someone speaking.

'It'll be light soon. Let's get moving.'

She opened her burning eyes to see it was Locke speaking. 'Think they will be on our trail yet?'

'Baxter is a hound dog,' Stickley replied. 'He will figure it out eventually, but he will have to backtrack until he finds where we left the trail. By us leaving the road on that hard rock surface it should take him some time to pick up our tracks.'

'So we have a half-day on the posse, maybe a little more or less?'

'Be my guess.'

'We have a lot of desert ahead,' Flint chimed in. 'Think we have enough water?'

'There are places to get water,' Locke replied. 'I've been down this way a time or two.'

'Oh, yeah,' Flint said, 'I remember you used to peddle some guns to the Mexicans, during their battle with the French.'

Locke uttered a sour grunt. 'Until they ended up stealing the guns from me because they couldn't pay. Lost most everything we had gained on that little venture.'

'Hence the reason to do business with your cousin, Flint,' Stickley said. 'We needed someone else to take the risks.'

'Hope Banty don't get himself kilt over this.'

'Your cousin knew the danger of doing business with us and the Indians.'

'Yeah, but if he's caught, he will sure enough end up with his neck in a noose for dealing guns to the Indians.'

'As will we all,' Locke told Flint.

'Enough chatter,' Stickley said. 'Roust your soft-headed girlfriend and let's get moving.' The toe of a boot jabbed Billy Jo on the back of her thigh. She lifted her head and blinked, as if she had been sound asleep.

'Let's go, honeycomb,' Flint said. 'With luck, you might see your special beau today.'

Billy Jo waited silently, while Flint removed the rope from her ankles. She had not been given any food or water, so she was unable to speak from the dryness in her throat. She felt too weak to move, but did manage to stand with his help. The pain shot up along her back and through her legs before she even attempted a step. Unable to suppress the urge she moaned from the discomfort.

'Yeah, I'm a little on the stiff side myself,' Flint told her. 'Sleeping on the ground gets harder as a man grows older.'

'Cut out the chatter and let's get moving!' Stickley ordered. 'It'll be daylight in a few minutes and we need to cover sixty miles before dark.'

Flint led Billy Jo over to her horse and helped her aboard. She sagged in the saddle and moaned softly from the renewed aches and pains. She wondered how long she could go without food or water. While in the cargo hold of the steamship she had nearly succumbed to her misery. She remembered being sick from bad food and tepid water, suffering the sweltering heat, the dank, musky smell and rank odor of rotten potatoes. If not for being discovered when Clay killed Lard, she might have died in that dark tomb.

However, Flint had said she might see Clay on this day. It was all she had to battle against the physical agony, the heat, dust, hunger and thirst. She clung to the thought, vowing to use her last bit of remaining strength to survive until she was again in his arms.

Grady was the better tracker of the two and Clay knew it. He relied on the savvy of his partner and followed his lead. By sunup the two of them were closing in on the Mexico border.

'Where do you think Baxter and the posse are at this morning?' Clay asked after a prolonged silence.

'If Flint's gal didn't steer us wrong on purpose, I'd guess he discovered they were on a false trail before sunset. With luck they might have picked up Locke's tracks before dark.'

'They will be a full day behind Stickley and us.'

'If the woman told you straight,' Grady repeated.

'Have you been down this way before?'

Grady bobbed his head. 'I rode with some of the soldier boys from Fort Yuma for a few days once, tracking a coupla killers. They robbed a bank in Phoenix and killed a soldier during the getaway. We worked together to catch up with them before they could reach the border.'

'I wonder if we shouldn't have contacted the commander at Fort Yuma and tried to get some help.'

'It would have taken us a couple of hours to get anything done, Val. I didn't think we had the time to spare. Besides, the two of us can handle those three jaspers.'

'Where would be the best place to cross into Mexico along here?'

'It's another few miles,' Grady replied. 'We'll try and find a place where we can keep watch. My concern is if they headed for California we might miss them.'

'And Baxter and his posse won't follow them across the border,' Clay added.

Grady paused to spit. He didn't chew to excess, but he did enjoy a chaw of tobacco on occasion. In the desert heat, it helped to keep the mouth and throat from drying out.

'If we don't get lucky today, we are going to have to pick up their tracks and follow their trail. It might take us a long time to catch up with them.'

'They took Billy Jo for a reason,' Clay told Grady. 'I can't imagine Stickley and Locke allowing Flint to bring along a hostage for his own company. Flint is a hired hand, while the judge and Locke ran the operation.'

'You think they will use her to barter with if we catch up with them?'

'It's the only thing which makes sense,'

Clay answered. 'I'm pretty sure the girl hasn't done much riding so she will slow them down.'

'Only if they care enough to allow her to slow them down, Val. As you pointed out, Stickley and Locke are in charge.'

'Let's pick up the pace, Grady. I've got a bad feeling about this chase.'

Locke's horse had begun to limp near mid-morning. By noon it was too crippled to walk. The four of them finally stopped near a lone mesquite. The tree had a few withered leaves and there were several dried pods lying about on the ground.

'This is as far as this nag is going,' Locke said. 'Guess we'll have to leave the girl here.'

Stickley took a long look over his shoulder, scanning the vista behind and to either side. There was no sign of anyone following.

'If the posse catches up, they will only have to load her on back of a horse and keep coming. The idea was to slow them down.'

'What's your thinking, Del?' Locke wanted to know.

Stickley tipped his head to Billy Jo. 'Transfer your gear to the girl's horse.'

Flint dismounted and pulled Billy Jo from the back of her horse while Locke began to strip the saddle from his lame animal. Stickley moved alongside of Locke and pulled his gun.

'They will have to spend more time if she is wounded,' he said.

Locke paused from his chore. 'A bullet in the leg would definitely slow them down. Might even stop a small posse.'

Flint stepped in front of Billy Jo and held out his hands, as if pushing against an invisible wall. 'Hold on now, boss,' he spoke to Locke. 'We can't go shooting a woman. We would have every marshal and bounty hunter in the country after us.'

'It will only be a small hole,' Stickley informed Flint. 'She might bleed a little, but it will give us the time we need.'

'And she might die too!' Flint objected a second time. 'What if they don't get here for a day or two? What if she gets infection and gangrene sets in?'

'We're running for our lives here, Flint,' Locke argued. 'We only have one chance to get out of this alive ... and she's the one who can give us that chance.'

But Flint did not move. 'I brought her into this, guys,' he said, begging for their understanding. 'It was my promises that brought her to Yuma. It ain't right she should be hurt on my account.'

Stickley gave a nod of agreement. 'You're right, Flint,' he said. 'It would be wrong to shoot an innocent girl just to slow down a posse.'

Flint lowered his hands and smiled. 'Sure thing, Judge. Those guys will still have to take it more slowly having her along. They won't catch us before we–'

But Stickley pulled the trigger!

Billy Jo gasped in surprise and shock, but the bullet had not been aimed at her. Flint buckled at the middle, his hands clutching his stomach. He sank to his knees and fell over onto his side, groaning in agony.

'A wounded man will have the same effect,' Stickley told Locke. 'They won't leave him here to die alone.'

Locke bobbed his head in agreement. 'And we don't have to split any money with him – more for us.'

The two men fixed a lead rope for Flint's horse and then left without another word, galloping away in a cloud of dust.

Billy Jo dragged Flint into the meager amount of shade from the mesquite tree. Without food or water she could do little to ease his pain.

Flint had been a scoundrel, a no good

louse, but he had prevented the judge from shooting her. Billy Jo removed her petticoat, tore a strip for a bandage, then folded the remainder for a pillow. After propping up Flint's head, she wrapped the strip of cloth around his waist and made it as tight as she could. Even so, the blood soaked through almost at once.

'Damn!' Flint muttered. 'I should have listened to Lotty.' He took a few ragged breaths, trying to manage the tremendous pain. 'She told me my weathercockism ways with women would sure enough be my demise.'

'Your...' Billy Jo had to take a moment to defeat the dryness of her mouth and throat, before she could get the words out. 'Your what?'

He tried to grin, but a spasm raked his body and he managed only a morbid grimace. 'A fancy word I heard one time for them who are fickle.'

'It's a more polite word than I would use for you,' Billy Jo said. 'You ran around the country seducing girls with your sweet words and kissing them, when you never had a serious bone in your body.'

Flint stifled a groan, waited for the misery to subside a bit and then gave his head a negative shake. 'You're wrong on that count, honeycomb. I was always serious about getting what I wanted.'

'So long as it wasn't permanent.'

'Well, Lotty was there to make sure I didn't have anything permanent with anyone else. If I would have had one decent bone in my body I would have married her.'

'We can agree on that.'

Flint stopped speaking, his teeth set against the waves of searing pain. It was only a matter of time and they both knew it.

It was the distant echo of a gunshot that stopped Grady and Clay. Without exchanging a word, they put their mounts into a ground-covering lope and headed toward the sound.

After a half-mile or so they spied a horse, standing near a lone mesquite. As they drew closer they could see someone on the ground.

Clay urged more speed, fearful Billy Jo had been shot and left to die.

Grady caught up as he began to pull back on the reins. They could now see the two people on the ground now – Billy Jo was kneeling over Flint Conner. Seeing them arrive, she jumped to her feet and raced for Clay.

Clay barely had time to dismount before she ran right into his arms. She buried her face in his shirt and cried against his chest.

'It ... it was supposed to be me lying there,' she explained between sobs. 'Flint stood between Stickley and me so the judge shot him instead. He said it would slow down a posse.'

'There's no posse, only Grady and I,' Clay said. 'The marshal and his men followed the tracks from town, in case we were wrong to head this way.'

She stepped back from him. 'But the judge and Locke are getting away!'

'Not to worry,' Grady spoke up. 'Val, you stay here and tend to the wounded man and your gal. I'll follow our two bucks until I can get 'em in my sights.'

'Don't take any chances,' Clay told his partner. 'We can run them to ground soon enough.'

'I didn't get this old by being careless,' Grady replied. He raised his hand in farewell and set off following the tracks of the three horses. Knowing he was only a few minutes behind, he would have to be careful.

Clay removed his canteen and offered it to Billy Jo. She drank greedily and then paused to lick her chapped lips. 'Um,' she murmured, 'and I thought the lemonade and ice was good!'

'How did you get here?' Clay asked.

'I'm sorry,' Billy Jo replied, handing him back the canteen. 'I went to the judge when I saw Flint and Locke getting ready to leave town. I thought he might know of a way to stop them.'

'And he turned out to be in league with our gun runners.'

'He was the number one man,' Flint gasped the words, suffering mightily from his stomach wound. 'Him and Locke were in the Confederate Army together.'

'Yes,' Billy Jo agreed, 'Locke was a sergeant and Stickley was a captain.'

'And they both double-crossed me,' Flint said bitterly.

The two of them moved over to shade the severely wounded man.

'He took the bullet meant for me.' Billy Jo said, her voice cracking with a sob.

'I wouldn't have been so gallant had I known you were within throwing distance, Valenteen.'

'Lotty didn't want you running off with another woman. She told us about your plan to leave a false trail and then head to Mexico.'

Flint was fading fast. His face was ashen,

his eyes became glazed and every breath was a ragged gulp. 'Good old Lot...' He coughed and doubled at the middle. After a few moments he rolled back, teeth tightly clenched, with sweat beading his brow. It took a heroic effort to manage to speak once more.

'Tell that cold-hearted, back-stabbing witch my final thoughts were of her.' He displayed a crooked grin. 'I'll be waiting for her in Hell!'

Clay almost replied to his wish, but Flint would not have heard the words. He had literally used up his last breath. The eyes were sightless, staring at the sky, while his jaw relaxed and his mouth fell open revealing uneven, tobacco-stained teeth.

With no extra horse and aware of what the summer heat could do to a corpse, Clay found a soft spot and scraped out a shallow grave. Once Flint was laid to rest, he and Billy Jo covered the burial spot with enough rocks to deter any wandering animals.

They had finished the chore and were debating rather to say words over his body when a rider appeared. It was Grady.

Clay and Billy Jo stood together to await his arrival. He had a grim expression on his face when he pulled his horse to a stop.

'Chase is over,' he told Clay. 'Chappabitty and some of his braves caught Locke and the judge. I guess they were a little displeased that no one showed up with their rifles.'

'Dead?' Clay asked.

'I arrived as the Indians rode off. They didn't leave enough for the buzzards to eat.'

Billy Jo took hold of Clay's hand and held it tightly. 'Those Indians weren't coming this way were they?'

Grady shook his shaggy head. 'Headed off toward Mexico. There weren't but six of them, not much of a raiding party.'

'Without the new rifles to entice more followers, the war chief is going to end up back on the reservation.'

'Or dead,' Grady said.

'Let's get headed back,' Clay said. 'It's going to be a long ride and the horses are already dragging.'

'You two ride double on your bronc for a spell and then we'll double on mine. If one of them don't come up lame, we should make it back to Yuma by sometime tomorrow.'

Clay gave an affirmative tip of his head. 'Can't be soon enough for us.'

The following morning they met up with Baxter and his posse. They had followed the false trail long enough to discover it was a phoney. Fortunately, they had two extra mounts to carry provisions. By transferring the supplies they freed up a horse for Billy Jo to ride. After that they made good time back to town.

Billy Jo wanted a bath so Clay and Grady went with the marshal to do the necessary paperwork to complete their job. As neither Locke nor Stickley had any known kin, their business enterprises were turned over to their perspective managers. Clay got a deposition stating the judge and his cohorts were all accounted for and out of the gun-running business for good. Then he headed over to send a wire to headquarters so he and Grady could be reassigned.

Billy Jo was luxuriating in her bath, relieving her tired and aching body when a tap came at her door.

'I'm in the tub!' she said. 'Go away!'

'Sorry,' Clay's voice came from the other side, 'but this won't wait. I'm coming in.'

Billy Jo leapt out of the tub like she had been fired out of a cannon. In one swift move she grabbed the blanket from the bed and wrapped it about her. She barely had time to catch a single breath before the door opened.

'Little britches?' Clay queried, poking his head through the crack. 'You decent?'

'More so than you!' she snapped. 'All I wanted was a few minutes to wash and to put on clean clothes so I could look nice for you.'

He eased the door open and entered the room. He carefully shut the door and smiled at her wet hair and bare shoulders. 'You look just fine, little britches,' he said. 'In fact, you were dressed much the same the first time I saw you as a woman at the jail.'

'You have such a keen memory,' she said tightly. 'Now, what is so important that it couldn't wait?'

'Two pieces of news.'

Billy Jo waited impatiently. 'I'm listening.'

'First, you don't have to worry about Jonas or Dutch any more. Threatened with going to prison, they withdrew the bounty and promised not to ever bother you again.'

That brightened her expression. 'Really?'

'Stickley actually did something right before he died.'

She laughed. 'Free at last!'

Clay enjoyed the sound of her mirth. He stood there enamored by the girl, admiring the way the blanket was just damp enough to cling to the contours of her body.

Billy Jo took notice of his stare and cleared

her throat. It helped to break his trance-like state. 'You said two bits of news,' she reminded him, lifting a single eyebrow.

'I wired my report and have been offered another job.'

'Another job?' Billy Jo appeared crest-fallen. 'You're leaving?'

'Yep,' he stated unequivocally. 'The job is in Denver and I start the first of next month.'

Billy Jo lowered her head. 'Denver?' she murmured.

'I'll be in charge of a number of agents and do most of my work out of an office.'

She still showed no enthusiasm. 'That sounds very nice for you.'

'You mean for *us*,' he corrected.

Billy Jo lifted her head to scrutinize Clay. 'Us?'

'Well, I am your legal guardian. I can't very well leave you here.'

She frowned. 'You mean you want to take care of me, as if I were still a child?'

Clay grinned. 'I was thinking of a more equal arrangement ... you know, a lifelong partnership?'

Billy Jo sprang across the room and threw her arms around Clay's neck. 'You want to marry me!' she declared.

Clay felt the damp warmth of her body against his as she kissed him soundly on the mouth. It wasn't until she pulled back that he could continue.

'I was getting to that part,' he gasped, out of breath from her kiss. 'I'd still be your guardian, just in a different way.'

She didn't answer in words. She kissed him again.

Clay decided some actions were decidedly more absolute than words. He enjoyed the girl in his arms and knew his trip to Yuma had been well worth the effort.